CANNIBAL JUNGLE

JON ATHAN

For more information on this book or the
author, please visit www.jon-athan.com.
General inquiries are welcome.

Facebook:
https://www.facebook.com/AuthorJonAthan
Twitter: @Jonny_Athan
Email: info@jon-athan.com

Book cover by Sean Lowery:
http://indieauthordesign.com/

Title page font (Horroroid) by Daniel
Zadorozny:
http://iconian.com/commercial.html

ISBN: 9781096052586

Thank you for the support!

WARNING

This book contains scenes of intense violence and some disturbing themes. Some parts of this book may be considered violent, cruel, disturbing, or unusual. This book is *not* intended for those easily offended or appalled. Please enjoy at your own discretion.

Table of Contents

Chapter One

Farewell

"When will you be back, dad?" Kyle Reed asked, a note of sadness in his voice.

Nathan Reed knelt down in front of his nine-year-old son. He looked the boy over, as if he didn't recognize his own kid. Kyle was anxious and afraid, but he wasn't *always* like that. He was a shy boy, the type to hide behind his mother in public, but he wasn't scared of people. It was something else, something nonhuman.

It was the big, monstrous airplane rolling down the taxiway and heading to the apron to refuel and pick-up the passengers.

Nathan felt a painful knot in his stomach due to his son's erratic behavior. He had a premonition of tragic, bloody disaster. It was supposed to be a normal goodbye: *'Don't worry, kiddo, I'll see you in a few weeks. Take care of your mother and be safe.'* At the moment, right there in Terminal B of the Los Angeles International Airport, he felt like he was saying his final farewells.

Nathan patted his son's shoulder and said, "I'll be back in about six weeks. Your mom will help you count each day."

"Of course I will," Holly Reed said as she looked down at their son. "I'm already counting, baby. Daddy will be back in... forty-five days."

Nathan said, "You see? Forty-five days. That's only a month and a half. That's nothing, kiddo. It'll be like I never left. Okay?"

"Okay," Kyle responded. He twiddled his fingers and twirled his hips. He said, "Will you bring me a present from Uru... Uru... Gay?"

"Uruguay. I'm going to Uruguay. And, *yes,* of course I'll bring you a present. It's going to be a surprise, though. You just have to wait for it. Can you wait for me?"

"Yeah, I guess so..."

"That doesn't sound very enthusiastic to me. You'll wait for me, right? You're not going to run off and find a new daddy, are you? Huh?"

Kyle giggled, then he said, "I'll wait for you."

Nathan grinned and said, "Attaboy. I'll be back before you know it. I promise."

He patted his shoulders again, then he kissed his forehead and hugged him. He stood up and did the same to his wife: a hug and a kiss.

"Will you be okay?" Kyle asked, just as his father reached for his carry-on. "Is it... Is it really safe?"

"What? The plane? Or Uruguay?"

"Both, I guess."

"I'll be fine, Kyle. It's like summer over there right now, so I might melt a little bit, but I'll come back in one piece."

Holly ruffled her son's feathery hair and said, "I can't wait until you take your first flight. You'll be mama's little baby again. So scared, so cute."

"I'm not scared," Kyle said, crossing his arms and shaking his head.

"Good," Nathan responded. "Now this is usually

the part where I say you're the man of the house. Well, you're not. So, I want you to listen to your mother. No ifs, ands, or buts. Do your homework, behave at home and at school, and *be safe.* Alright? Good. I love you, kiddo. Come on, give dad another hug."

Nathan and Kyle shared another long, warm hug. Nathan turned his attention to his wife. She smiled, she looked confident, but her pupils were dim. She was worried, too.

She said, "Be careful out there, hun. Seriously, you don't know what kind of animals and insects are over there. I mean, imagine running into one of those huge spid–"

"Don't even say it," Nathan interrupted, his eyes closed in mock frustration. "You know I *hate* spiders. I don't even want to think about it. Shit, Holly, now I won't be able to sleep for the entire flight."

"You better sleep a little," Holly said as she closed in on him, her face a mere foot away from his chest. "I want a *long*, 'romantic' call with you when you land. Okay? Alright?"

"Romantic? Do you mean what I think you mean?"

Holly smirked and whispered, "Yes."

They shared another long, passionate kiss. Although they were in their mid-thirties, they resembled a young couple in a long-distance relationship at an airport. They couldn't keep their hands off each other.

Nathan pulled away from the kiss, grabbed his bag, and said, "Alright, I really have to go. I love you. You hear me, Kyle? I love the both of you." As he walked away, he shouted, "Wait for me! I'll be back!"

"We love you, too," Holly said as she waved at him.

Kyle waved, jumped, and shouted, "Don't melt, dad!"

Holly's final words warmed his heart. It was true and he knew it well. Kyle's gentle voice and silly message put a smile on his face. He walked up to the security checkpoint, ready to head to his gate.

***

Nathan took a deep breath as the plane roared down the runway. He heard rumbling, groaning, and the occasional *thud.* Although weak and barely perceptible, he felt his seat vibrating. It felt like the beginning of a roller coaster ride—the scariest ride in the world. His eyes widened as the plane rose from the ground. He closed the window shade in a haste and looked at the screen on the headrest in front of him.

He drew another deep breath, trying his best to calm his nerves. He acted strong and confident in front of his family for *their* sake, but the mere thought of flying terrified him. He remembered the tragic events he saw on the news: planes crashing into building in acts of shocking terrorism, being blown out of the sky by Russian missiles, vanishing into thin air over seemingly endless seas, plummeting to the ground shortly after takeoff. Anything could happen in the sky, and he felt like he had no control over it.

"First time flying, ay?" a man said.

Nathan sighed and glanced over at the neighboring seat. A middle-aged man sat beside him, his slick hair graying and his tanned skin wrinkling. He was big, his stomach was soft, but he was undoubtedly strong. A blue U-shaped pillow around his neck, he looked comfortable and happy on the plane. He wasn't scared of flying. It looked like he wasn't scared of anything.

Nathan responded, "It's not my first time, actually. I've done it before and I'll do it again. I just... I don't like it. I never got used to it, I guess."

"Really? Well, you gotta do what you gotta do," the man said. He extended his arm towards Nathan for a handshake. He said, "The name's Cole Hudson. It's a pleasure to meet you."

"It's, um... It's nice to meet you, too. My name is Nathan. Nathan Reed."

"So, Nathan, are you going on vacation?"

"Nope."

"Yeah, I figured, but it seemed like a good, safe question to start with. You don't seem like the type, you know? A little too... 'uptight.' But not in a bad way. Please don't take it personally."

Nathan smiled, shrugged, and said, "Don't worry about it. Nervous, uptight, stressed. I'm all of the above right now."

"I can see that," Cole responded. "You should consider taking a real long break. Me? I'm heading to São Paulo for my vacation. I've been there dozens of times in my life, but it feels like the first time every time. An amazing, gorgeous city with arguably the richest culture in the world. I might buy another home out there. I just might make it my retirement home."

Nathan examined the man from head-to-toe. Cole wore a plain polo shirt, cargo shorts, and slippers with dress socks. He didn't look wealthy, but he gave off a wealthy aura. He reminded him of some of the young billionaires he saw in interviews—plenty of money with simple, minimalistic fashion. Suits and ties didn't equal wealth after all.

He said, "I hope you don't mind me asking, but what do you do, Cole?"

Cole chuckled, then he said, "Mind? Do I mind? Hell, Nathan, I'm *glad* you asked. Now, it might not be obvious to you from the surface, I might seem like the shy-type based off my looks, but I love speaking. I especially love speaking about myself. And I'm not saying that in a conceited way. I just feel like... if I open up, then *you'll* open up or *he'll* open up or *she'll* open up. We learn from each other and we grow from our learning. Talking, communication... It's important, man."

Nathan couldn't help but smile as he cocked his head to the side. The gesture said something along the lines of: *what the hell are you talking about?* He was amused by Cole's rambling. He didn't seem like the shy-type at all. He understood his point and he agreed with him, but it all sounded so bizarre in the airplane.

Cole continued, "So, let me tell you what I do. I'm what you call an 'entrepreneur.' I guess you can say I've stuck my finger into every pie. The dot-com bubble, real estate, Bitcoin, cannabis, phone apps, social networks... I've invested in the people I believed in, and it paid off most of the time. If I didn't communicate with the people around me, I wouldn't be in my position today."

"Your position? Your position in, um, economy

class?" Nathan responded as he grabbed his laptop from under the seat in front of him. He looked back at Cole and said, "I don't mean any offense by that or anything like that. It's just that you're talking big game and I was wondering why a successful man like yourself would be back here with an *unsuccessful* man like me."

"No offense taken, man. I get it. I don't look rich. Hell, I probably don't sound rich, either. I don't like flaunting my wealth. I hate doing that, actually. It's not guilt or shame, I just find it annoying and distasteful. More importantly, I like being around people. People like you, Nathan. I don't want to pick your brain or steal your ideas, but I want to hear your voice. Communication made me successful, so I want to communicate. Up there, up in 'first class' or whatever you want to call it, it's usually quiet. They don't want to talk like we're talking now. And there aren't as many people in that cabin, either. I think it's pretty damn lonely. That's not my style. Nope, it's just not for me."

Nathan stared at him, eyes shining with curiosity. He believed every word out of his mouth. He didn't know what to say, so he nodded at him. He opened his laptop and clicked through a few documents. He caressed his short brown beard and ran his fingers through his long hair, as if he were thinking deeply about something.

Constantly glancing at Nathan's computer, Cole asked, "So, what about you? You're traveling on business, right? What do you do if you don't mind me asking?"

"I work in telecommunications," Nathan said, eyes stuck on his monitor.

"In São Paulo?"

"No, no. I'm heading to Uruguay for a business opportunity."

"How long?"

Hmm—Nathan let out the sound through his sealed lips as he peeked over at Cole.

"How long's your trip?" Cole clarified.

"Oh. About six or seven weeks."

"Damn. That's a long time away from home," Cole responded. He frowned as he spotted Nathan's wedding ring. He asked, "What does your family think?"

Nathan glared at him. The men met less than ten minutes ago. They weren't best friends, they weren't even regular acquaintances. He didn't expect to see Cole again after landing in São Paulo, so he didn't feel comfortable sharing details from his personal life— especially since those details concerned his wife and son.

He said, "My family *knows* I'm doing what's best for us. I love my wife, I love my son, and I know they love me. That's all there is to it. Okay?"

Cole bit his lip and raised his hands up to his chest—*sorry, my mistake.* Nathan typed away on his laptop, trying his best to focus on his work. The letters and numbers on the document appeared to be jumbled together. He blinked once, twice, and then thrice. He could only see one word on the page: *bankruptcy.* He squeezed his eyes shut. Upon opening his eyes once more, he saw a regular document.

Cole said, "You probably don't need advice from a

stranger on a plane, but... like I said, I enjoy speaking. So, let me tell you something. Climbing up the ladder of success is great, but I think you'll find plenty of happiness where you're at now. You might even be in the perfect position already. A wife, a kid... Sometimes, it feels like I have all of the money in the world, but I can't buy what you have. Cherish them when you get back. Don't ever go six or seven weeks without seeing them again. Okay? It's not always about the money, you know?"

Nathan gazed into Cole's glittering blue eyes. He wanted to say: *it's easy for you to say that when you have gold coins falling out of your pockets—and your ass.* But he felt the sincerity in his message. Cole meant no harm with his prying or his advice. He only wanted Nathan to learn from his mistakes.

The sound of boisterous laughter interrupted their moment.

Nathan glanced over at the back of the cabin. He saw Mariah Henderson—a twenty-two-year-old woman—shushing her cackling friend as she smiled and snickered. The women looked happy, but he didn't think she was as wealthy as Cole.

He scanned the rest of the cabin. He saw people from all backgrounds—elderly men and women, families and couples, young adults and teenagers, children and babies. Some of them slept, others chatted amongst themselves, and a few watched movies on their seatback screens. The economy class cabin was filled with happiness.

Nathan said, "I appreciate the advice, but it's not that easy. It's not about making a million dollars or a billion or a trillion. I want to bring happiness to my wife and my son. I know money can't buy happiness, I've heard all of the cautionary tales, but money can buy shelter, transportation, food, education, and insurance. I *need* this to get our lives back on track. When I finish this, when I–I've taken control of our finances… then I can stay with my family. That's the plan, at least. I have to do this."

Cole clenched his jaw and puckered his lips. He understood and accepted Nathan's point of view. He thought about offering his assistance—a job opportunity, a small loan, investment advice, *anything.* But he didn't want to intrude. He couldn't save someone who wasn't asking for rescue. He pulled a business card out of his wallet and handed it to Nathan.

He said, "Give me a call sometime. We can talk business or we can chat about life. Either way, I think it'll be productive."

Nathan smiled and nodded at him. He was comforted by Cole's genuine kindness and concern. He couldn't stop himself from grinning, even as he stared at his monitor and continued working.

***

Nathan swayed from side-to-side and bounced in his seat. His eyes snapped open and nearly popped out of his head. He looked down at himself. He felt his seat vibrating, as if he were sitting on a massage chair. He glanced over at the seatback screen in front of him. It was minuscule, barely perceptible to the human eye, but he swore he saw the screen moving.

He stretched his neck up and examined the dark cabin. Stewardesses walked down the aisles and handed out burritos, yogurt, fruit, and beverages. Some passengers waited near the restroom, but most of them remained seated. Cole wore an eye mask and earplugs as he slept in his seat, his chin on his chest and a drop of gooey drool hanging from his bottom lip.

Nathan shook Cole's shoulder and said, "Hey. Hey, wake up. Did I miss any announcements or–"

The plane shook, but the episode lasted longer than before—and it was much, *much* stronger. It felt like a powerful earthquake, but the plane was 40,000 feet above the ground. Some of the overhead bins popped open. A duffel bag fell to the floor, quickly followed by a large purse. An older gentleman lost his footing and landed on his ass near the restroom. He laughed it off, along with the other passengers.

The shaking was mistaken for normal turbulence. The laughter stopped as soon as the passengers heard a *ding*. The seatbelt symbol lit up. Then an announcement followed.

The stewardess said, "Ladies and gentlemen, the captain has warned of turbulent weather. For your safety, please return to your seats and fasten your seatbelts immediately. Do not move around the cabin while the seatbelt sign is on. Do not–"

The entire plane shook again. The lights flickered on and off. Bags of all shapes and sizes poured out of the overhead bins. A man lurched down an aisle, bumping into everyone on his way down to the floor. A woman shrieked in the restroom. A young stewardess strapped herself to her seat, her cheeks wet with fresh tears.

His voice strained from the stress, the captain made an announcement: "Ladies and gentlemen, please fasten your seatbelts *now.* We're entering a massive storm and we expect some severe turbulence. I–I've never seen anything like this before. I... I am going to attempt to fly over it now. Stay seated and be ready to brace for impact. If you're religious, please pray for us."

"Oh my God," a young woman shouted. "Oh my God!"

"It's going to be okay, just keep your head down," a man said, trying his best to comfort his frightened son. "It's just turbulence. This happens on every flight. It's normal."

Nathan's breathing intensified, his hands and limbs trembled, and tears filled his eyes. He awoke from a dream and landed in a nightmare. His clammy hands slid across the straps of his belt as he struggled to fasten it.

"Fuck, shit, fuck, damn it," he muttered.

Cole grabbed his wrist with a gentle grip. Nathan looked him in the eye. He felt a sudden sense of security, as if he were gazing into his father's eyes.

Cole said, "Everything is going to be okay, Nathan. This happens a lot out here. It's just a tropical storm. Take a deep breath, fasten your seatbelt, and relax. You can do this."

Nathan nodded in agreement as he followed Cole's directions. He drew a deep breath through his nose, then he fastened his seatbelt. He looked at the window to his right. He closed his eyes and whimpered as he felt the plane ascending—shaking but ascending. He told himself to ignore the window, he knew nothing good would come from peeking, but he had to know the truth.

His eyes widened as he opened the window shade and looked outside. A bolt of lightning illuminated the dark skies with a short, vibrant blue glow. The sound of thunder burst into the plane, louder than the rumbling engines and panicking passengers. They were *in* the storm, craggy bolts of lightning dancing around them and rain pattering against the steel.

Nathan closed the window shade. He looked at Cole, who sat in the brace position—bent forward at the waist, hands over the back of his head, his head close to the seat in front of him.

His head down, Cole asked, "Are you listening? You do it like this, okay?"

"*What?*" Nathan asked, baffled.

During his episode of fear, he didn't realize Cole was trying to teach him how to survive. He didn't hear his voice. The plane trembled, rocking from side to side. The aircraft even dipped down before it ascended again. Bags rose from the floor, then they plummeted, and then they rose from the floor again, like basketballs on a court.

Through another announcement, the pilot said, "We need you to brace for impact. This is a precautionary measure, but we need you to brace. Please follow the cabin crew's instructions."

The stewardesses and stewards repeated the same term over and over: *Brace, brace, brace! Brace, brace, brace!*

The lights went out inside of the plane. Red

emergency lights illuminated the aisles and the areas between the cabins. Oxygen masks fell from the compartments over the seats. The passengers cried and scream while sitting in the brace position. Some of them recorded the event on their cell phones, others tried to grab their belongings from the floor. The instructions from the cabin crew were drowned out by the pandemonium.

Nathan couldn't stop himself from hyperventilating. He grabbed the oxygen mask and tried to put it on. The band kept slipping out of his fingers. He heard Cole's voice and he saw his lips flapping, but he didn't understand his words. It sounded like: *Nathan, don't panic.* But it looked like: *Nathan, you're dying.*

Before he could say a word, his pupils dilated with fear and his nose scrunched up into a bundle of ridges. He caught a whiff of smoke. He opened the window shade and looked outside.

"Oh no," he whispered in awe.

Black smoked billowed out of the engine under the wing. The flash from a bolt of lightning surged past the smoke, then the thunder roared towards the plane. Flames crackled and popped in the engine and the fire emitted an orange light. The plane tilted to the right and began to turn, then it slowly descended.

Nathan felt his heart pounding against his chest as he saw the endless forest several miles below him— 40,000 feet, 39,000 feet, *35,000 feet below.* He pictured the plane nosediving straight into the ground.

But, before the plane could drop any farther, the engine exploded. The broken engine plummeted away from the plane. Flames swallowed the wing, hot enough to persevere through the rain, and danced up to the fuselage of the plane. The light from the fire illuminated every inch of Nathan's contorted, terrified face.

"Brace! Nathan, brace!" Cole shouted as he tugged on Nathan's arm.

Nathan finally heard his voice. He heard the rest of the chaos in the cabin, too. He levitated a centimeter from his seat, but the seatbelt kept him from hovering away. He felt his stomach sink as the plane descended. Then, he felt a pint of vomit climbing up his throat. Dark brown goop burst out of his mouth. For a second, it looked like it was floating in mid-air in front of him. The vomit hit his face, his clothes, and the seat.

He yelled, "Oh my God! No! No, please, no!"

He kept screaming—blurts of incomprehensible noise—as he looked around the plane. It was the most horrific event he had ever witnessed.

The passengers shrieked in terror, vocal cords tearing in the process. He heard praying in several different languages—English, Spanish, Hindi. Some of the passengers recorded videos for their families and others attempted to call their loved ones, frantically tapping their phones while trying to keep their devices steady.

There was no signal out there. Their calls and their messages—their final goodbyes—would never be sent or received.

A young, raven-haired girl—about seven years old—slipped out of her seatbelt and flew up. Her weeping stopped as soon as the top of her head collided with the ceiling of the cabin. The *thud* of the impact could be heard over the chaos. The blow was strong enough to crack her skull. Her eyes immediately hemorrhaged, turning blood-red within seconds.

Then her limp, unconscious body soared down the aisle, as if it were floating on the surface of a fast-flowing river, bouncing from one overhead bin to the other. She went past the restrooms and entered the next cabin.

Horrified by her daughter's injuries, the girl's mother acted hastily. She unbuckled her belt, which launched her from her seat. She let out a bloodcurdling scream as she was flung across the cabin. Mid-air, she collided with another woman—head-to-head. The *thump* of their collision was accompanied by a hair-raising *crunching* sound.

Their necks simultaneously snapped. The concerned mother hit the wall at the end of the cabin between the aisles, the other woman was caught between a row of seats.

An elderly man towards the center of the cabin banged on the window with the bottom of his fist. He adjusted the oxygen mask over his face while scratching at his neck. The oxygen mask's bag didn't inflate, and that made him panic. He felt the oxygen hitting his thin, crusty lips, but he couldn't draw a satisfying breath.

Voice muffled by the mask, he yelled, "Help! I can't breathe! I can't breathe! Meryl! Meryl, honey! I can't breathe! Please, Lord, help me!"

His fingernails sliced into his neck. The first cuts

were thin and short. He drove his fingernails into his throat again. The lacerations were deeper and longer. He inadvertently cut into one of his jugulars. Geysers of blood shot out in short, rapid bursts. The blood burst forward towards the seat in front of him, but then the droplets flew back and struck his face.

Like a drug addict itching for another hit, he couldn't stop himself from scratching his neck. His survival instincts told him to make a hole in his throat since he couldn't breathe from his nose or mouth. He clawed at his throat until his thyroid hung out of his neck.

The bathroom door burst open and a woman flew out, her pants around her knees. She was slammed against the parallel bathroom, then she hit the ceiling. She scratched at the walls, but she couldn't stop herself from falling into the other cabin. Her head was sliced by an open overhead bin, the cut stretching from her left temple to the back of her skull.

She grabbed the overhead bin's door, sobbing and screeching, but to no avail. The door snapped off its hinges and she fell towards the center of the plane. Her screaming was lost in a concert of shrieks from the other loose passengers. More bags flew out of the overhead bins, raining down on the passengers and soaring through the cabins.

The other engine malfunctioned, igniting into a ball of flames. The fan's sharp blades flew in every direction. One of the blades tore through the side of one of the cabins, ripping through the steel and shattering the windows. In a flash, six passengers were decapitated. One of the shorter passengers—a middle-aged woman—had her head split in half horizontally at the bridge of her nose by the blade. The top half of her head fell on her lap, eyes wide open.

Nathan tightened his grip on the armrests as the plane took a sharp right. The plane's descent accelerated.

"No, no, no, no, no," Nathan muttered.

The sound of *clanking* and *clunking* steel echoed through the plane. Another explosion towards the center of the plane lit up the cabins, but Nathan couldn't see the source. He closed his eyes and screamed. The heat from the explosion warmed his face—warm, hot, *blistering.* He feared his face would melt off his skull. Then a cool breeze caressed his skin.

He opened his eyes and watched as the front half of the plane disconnected from the back half. He saw passengers—elderly, adult, young, adolescent, newborn—falling from the clouds like raindrops.

Cole shouted, "Brace! Brace, Nathan!"

Nathan stared ahead vacantly, paralyzed by fear. His half of the plane entered a thick forest, slipping between trees and bulldozing through branches. Their luck didn't last long. The left half of the cabin was torn off as they crashed into a sturdy tree trunk. The volume of the screaming decreased in an instant—death happened in the blink of an eye.

Nathan winced and sobbed as he heard an explosion behind him. He couldn't tell if it came from the other half of the cabin, the front half of the plane, or his cabin. He only knew things were exploding around him. His head hit the window and he instantly lost consciousness. The cabin, crumbling piece by piece, fell deeper into the jungle.

Chapter Two

The Great Amazonia

Nathan sniffled as he opened his eyes. His vision was unfocused, as if he had just exited a dungeon after several lightless days. He saw a bright white light, blotches of green and blue, and floaters—squiggly lines in his eyesight. He clenched his eyes shut, then he opened them, and then he closed them again. He repeated the process until the white light dimmed.

He recognized it: *a ray of sunshine*. He felt a breeze against his sweaty face and neck. He tried to inhale deeply—to savor the fresh air, to appreciate his survival—but the breath caused a jolt of burning pain to surge across his torso. He feared his lungs were pierced by a branch. He tapped his chest and he didn't feel any cuts.

He breathed again—*ow!*

Tears trickled from his eyes, but he couldn't see them land. He breathed in short breaths and tried to minimize the pain. He whimpered as he stared down at himself. He could barely see the outline of his body. He recognized his gray button-up shirt, his dark blue jeans, and his dress socks. He lost his boots during the crash. His clothing looked sooty and tattered. He knew something was wrong.

"No, God, no. My ribs... My ribs are broken. Oh, shit, they're broken," he whispered. He looked every which way and yelled, "Help! Somebody–"

He coughed and hissed in pain. Although he

couldn't control it, the coughing only caused more pain to reverberate through his body. He cracked a rib or two during the plane crash. The pain from each breath was irritating, but he figured he got off better than the others. Images of children falling from the sky—some on fire, some already dead—flashed in his mind.

He looked to his left. The other seat was still attached to his, but Cole was missing. He held his breath as he noticed the thick, gnarled tree trunk next to Cole's seat.

"Shit, I'm... I'm on a... a..."

Tree.

I'm on a tree.

He heard those words in his head, he could even visualize every letter, but he couldn't say it. If he said it, he feared it would make it true. He looked down at himself again. His peripheral vision was still blurred, but he could finally see. And he saw his legs dangling under him, about ten meters above the muddy ground. As pale as milk, he grabbed the armrests and leaned back against his seat.

It's not real, I'm not stuck in a fucking tree, he told himself. *I'm still on the plane. I'm just dreaming and I have to wake up, right?*

He gasped as the seats shook and the branches groaned under him. Two branches caught the seats during the crash and stopped them from hitting the floor—*splat!* Those branches couldn't hold his weight forever, though. He thought about his options: sit and wait until the branches gave out or jump and face the problem head-on.

He whispered, "Okay, I might not be dreaming. I

need to... to do something. I need–"

"Nathan," a voice interrupted.

Nathan's grip on the armrests loosened. He heard a calm, smooth voice—*Cole's voice.* He leaned forward carefully and looked down.

Cole leaned against a tree, using a branch as a crutch. He dropped a duffel bag between his feet and he carried a plastic water bottle in his hand. His salmon-colored polo shirt was torn, a sleeve hanging down to his gut. His left eye was swollen shut, purple and red. There were tiny cuts across his arms and face. It looked like he had crawled through a field of broken glass.

Cole said, "Be careful coming down from there. I busted my ankle when I jumped down. Shit, I don't know if I just twisted it or shattered every damn bone in there. I'm telling you: be *very* careful."

Nathan asked, "Wha–What happened? How did we–"

"Come down and we'll talk."

"I–I'm scared, Cole."

"I know you are. I'm scared, too. But you're better off down here than up there. Besides, sooner or later, those seats are going to come crashing down. Come on, man, you can do it."

Nathan nodded reluctantly. He unbuckled his belt, then he scooted forward until he sat at the edge of his seat. From those branches, ten meters looked like ten miles. The muddy ground directly under him looked soft, though.

Cole said, "I wish I could catch you, but I'd probably throw out my back or break my leg if I tried.

I'm sorry, man."

"Don–Don't worry about it. I'm going to, um… I'm going to jump now, alright?"

"Alright, I'm waiting for you."

Nathan took a deep breath, causing him to grimace and hiss. His clammy palms slipped off the armrests, then his ass slid off the seat. He screamed as he fell to the ground. The shouting didn't last longer than a second. He landed on his feet and rolled away from the trunk. He thought his chest was about to burst because of the pain emanating from his broken ribs, although his legs were unharmed during the landing.

Sobbing and mumbling incoherently, he rolled onto his back and stared up at the sky. The trees stretched into a morning sky of orange, blue, and gray, reaching into the heavens—so tall. The branches waved at him with each gust of wind. Birds chirped from the branches, small critters scampered from one bush to another, and monkeys *eeked* and *hooed* from seemingly everywhere. He spotted a green iguana strutting near a tree stump and a toucan on a branch. The forest was filled with so much life.

But it was also filled with the remnants of an explosive tragedy. The jungle was bestrewn with broken pieces of the airplane. Blankets of black smoke rolled skyward from the burning pieces. Dead bodies littered the forest, too. Some of the bodies were stuck in the trees, others hit the ground or landed in rivers, and a few were still stuck in their seats.

"Holy shit," he muttered as he struggled to his feet.

He staggered towards Cole. He placed his palm on the same tree as him and caught his breath. He breathed slowly and carefully so as not to aggravate his cracked ribs. He stared at Cole and Cole stared back at him. They couldn't translate their emotions into words.

They were grateful to be alive, but they couldn't just walk away from a plane crash as if nothing had happened. Hundreds of lives were lost, consequently affecting *thousands* of their friends and relatives directly. The tragedy would surely ripple across the globe, touching hundreds of thousands of people through social media and news outlets.

If the survivors weren't found, the headline would read: *flight bound for São Paulo crashes, all 237 on board killed.* Nathan and Cole didn't want to face that headline. Post-traumatic stress disorder, survivor's guilt, anxiety, depression—their minds were already being flooded with the most pessimistic thoughts. Their gratefulness couldn't cure their broken hearts.

Nathan held his hand over his face and sobbed. He leaned forward, his forehead against Cole's shoulder. The pain from his ribs suddenly felt appropriate. Cole took a step back and clenched his teeth because of the pain coming from his leg. He didn't push him away, though. He knew Nathan was young and he had a lot to lose, so he let him cry. He didn't know how to process the situation himself, either.

Nathan struck the tree with the bottom of his fist and yelled, "What happened?! What the hell happened? Like... what the fuck, Cole? *What the fuck?!*"

He crossed his arms over his stomach, bent forward, and groaned. The grief and anguish were overwhelming.

Cole patted his back gently and said, "Hey, it's okay. Everything's going to be okay."

"*How?!* How, Cole? Everyone... everyone is dead."

"But you're not. Hundreds of people are dead and that's a damn tragedy, but you survived, Nathan. We landed in a... a green hell, but we're the lucky ones. Can't you see that? You *will* get to see your family again. I'll make sure of that. Okay?"

Nathan nodded and swiped at the glob of mucus dribbling over his lips. He was reinvigorated by the mere thought of his wife and son, Holly and Kyle. He trusted Cole, too. He glanced around the jungle. *Hundreds of people are dead*—Cole's words echoed through his head. Tainting the scent of nature, he caught a whiff of smoke, gasoline, and death.

Death had a powerful scent—the more tragic the death, the more powerful the scent. A stench, like charcoal, sulfur, and bodily gasses blended together, wafted through the jungle. It was the scent of burning muscle, fat, and hair. It was a repugnant stench, staining *everything* in the area. Nothing could mask the scent—nothing in the world.

Nathan saw the carnage in Cole's good eye, playing back on his cornea like video through a projector. The man tried to stay positive, but he witnessed something horrible during the crash.

Nathan asked, "So what do we do now?"

"We survive."

"Survive? Yeah, okay, um... That's obvious, but you make it sound easy. Have you ever been in a situation like this?"

Cole took a swig of his water, then he furrowed his

brow and asked, "Have I ever survived a plane crash?"

"No. I mean, have you ever survived anything like this? You ever been stranded in the middle of nowhere? You ever... You ever survive against wilderness?"

Cole handed him the water bottle. He said, "Take a drink, but don't chug it. We have to pace ourselves. It can be the difference between life and death. Now, to answer your question, I've never been in a situation like this. I've camped, I've hiked, but I've never done the whole 'man versus nature'-thing. I've only ever seen it in movies, TV, and video games. But, I figure common sense should keep us alive."

Nathan took a sip of water and looked up at the trees. He saw a pair of spider monkey swinging through the trees, using their long limbs and prehensile tails to move effortlessly. He saw monkeys in zoos, but he had never seen a spider monkey in its natural habitat. He wondered if he could really survive out there.

His eyes on the monkeys, he asked, "So what does your common sense say we should do right now? Other than survive?"

"My common sense is telling me: find clean, drinkable water; build shelter and a fire; and then find food. I don't think we have to worry about food too much, though. We can survive a couple of days without a full meal. We'll be rescued before we starve, I guarantee that. We can't live long without drinking water, though. And the fire... I think it'll be hot out here at night, it's hot as hell now, but we'll still need a fire to keep the animals away. That's what my common sense is telling me. How does that sound?"

"It sounds promising, I guess. We don't need food because they're looking for us, right? It was a–a–a commercial aircraft, right? Those just don't crash and disappear, they're not just reported and forgotten the next day. A rescue team should be coming soon. Yeah, they're not just going to leave us out here like this."

"That's what I'm talking about, Nathan. You have to look at the bright side. We can…"

Nathan stopped listening to Cole's voice. He found himself staring at a toucan as pessimistic thoughts crept into his mind.

His voice low and raspy, he said, "But… we crashed during a storm." Cole stopped speaking. Nathan continued, "I don't think we had wi-fi during most of that flight. What if we were disconnected from the rest of the world when we crashed? If the wi-fi didn't work, was the GPS working? What if another storm swallows this whole damn area? They'll wait a few days before they start searching, won't they? Maybe even a few weeks, right? We have no *fucking* idea where we landed, so why would anyone else know? We're–"

"Stop it," Cole interrupted. "You start thinking like that and you'll go crazy. 'What if this? What if that?' What-ifs are rarely helpful, Nathan. We need to focus on the task at hand. Water, shelter, fire, food. And, who knows? Maybe we'll find other survivors out there. It seems unlikely, sure, but we're living proof that miracles can happen. Either way, my point stands: we have to start surviving."

Nathan gripped the chest of his shirt and drew a deep breath. The stinging pain from his rib cage persisted. He examined Cole's condition. Cole couldn't see from his swollen eye, his body was covered in lacerations, and his ankle was purple and inflamed. They were disoriented and injured.

Nathan glanced up at the cabin seats on the tree branches. He said, "I'm not sure we should be moving around after... *that.* We're not dead, but we're injured. And, besides, wouldn't it make it harder for a rescue team to find us if we wander off? If they're even looking..."

Cole responded, "We don't have a lot of options. In this heat, this water won't last us more than a day. Sure, we can hope they rescue us in the next twenty-four hours, but that's risky. And you're right: we're injured. *But,* if I can limp around with this busted ankle and find these supplies, then moving through this jungle will be a breeze for you." He patted Nathan's shoulder and said, "We have one chance to survive. If we fail out here, we die. Every choice matters, every minute matters. I'm with you, Nathan. Okay? I am with you. But you have to think about this, and you can't let fear control you. So, what do you want to do?"

Nathan thought about his options. Thanks to Cole's speech, wait-and-see sounded like wait-and-die. He didn't want to move, he was terrified, but he knew it was his best bet.

He nodded at Cole, as if to say: *let's go.*

Chapter Three

The Lucky Ones

Nathan and Cole traversed the jungle, limping through thick bushes, trudging through swaths of mud, and dodging the animals in their natural habitats. They followed the smoke, heading to the plane's debris in hopes of finding supplies and other survivors. They figured the rescue teams would be drawn to the smoke as well. They didn't want to miss their flight out of the jungle.

The problem was: the burning wreckage was scattered across *dozens* of square miles of dense vegetation. The debris and the bodies were thrown around like farms and cows in a tornado.

As he led the way, grimacing and groaning with each step, Cole said, "I've walked through... here before. After I dropped from those seats, I tried to... look for water and supplies on my own. I couldn't go far, though. It was... It was too damn dark. But we're lucky it's summer down here in the southern hemisphere. If it were winter... we probably would have frozen in our sleep."

"How far did you go?" Nathan asked, following closely behind him. The duffel bag slung over his shoulder got caught on every twig and vine, slowing him down every step of the way, but he kept up with Cole. He said, "I mean, before I woke up. Where did you go? What did you see? How long was I, um, *out?*"

"Like I said, I couldn't go far. My ankle was killing

me, it was dark, and I didn't want to stray too far away from you. I knew that I needed to be around when you woke up."

"Yeah, thanks for that."

"No problem," Cole said. He sighed, leaned against a tree, and took a gander at his surroundings. He said, "We've already gone farther than I did earlier. I found that bag and water near our seats. I found some woman's clothes over there, right in that bush. I didn't find any women, though. I screamed for help, but... Yeah, I didn't see anyone."

Nathan sensed the sadness in Cole's voice. He was saddened by the tragedy, too. He held his hand over his chest and cried. For a second, he thought his heart actually broke. He felt the warm blood oozing out of his heart and spreading across his torso. Then he remembered about his cracked ribs.

In a strained voice, Nathan said, "Cole... Cole, I need help."

"What? What's wrong?"

"I think my ribs are broken. Every time I breathe, it feels like my chest is going to explode. *Every. Time.* It hurts so fuckin' bad. Can you help me? Do you know how to fix this?"

Cole shook his head and said, "Sorry, pal, I have no idea how to fix a broken bone. If I did, I wouldn't be walking around with a busted ankle. But I know painkillers will help. Someone must have had some ibuprofen or Vicodin or *something* on that plane. We just need to find it. Keep your eyes peeled for any luggage. Now let's get moving. We can't stay here forever."

Nathan followed Cole through the jungle. Their

movements were slow and meticulous. They were already injured, so they couldn't risk harming themselves any further. The music of nature surrounded them—rustling leaves, creaking bushes, yelping animals, chirping insects. They spotted a three-toed sloth hanging from a tree, looking relaxed.

Under any other circumstances, the men would have felt compelled to photograph the sloth—maybe even take a selfie with the mammal. In the jungle, fighting for survival against nature and their own human frailty, they saw a meal. The same question ran through their minds: *what does sloth meat taste like?*

They kept walking.

They couldn't see the smoke through the tall trees, so they followed the scent of smoke and death. The stench became more putrid as they approached the first fire. Then, they heard the *crackling* of the flames. Plumes of black smoke danced through the jungle, undulating between the trees above them. They were getting closer to the crash site—*closer, closer.*

"Jesus Christ," Cole muttered as he squeezed past a bush and a tree. His eye wide with fear and his face scrunched in disgust, he repeated, "*Jesus Christ.*"

As he approached from behind, Nathan asked, "What is it? Are they–"

He stopped speaking upon spotting the wreckage. There were no survivors in sight. There was no sign of life in the immediate area, as a matter of fact. The jungle's animals moved away from the fire—from the death.

A piece of the plane—slanted like a ramp—burned

in front of them, partially submerged in a pit of mud. It was a piece of one of the economy cabins. Three rows of seats were still attached to the bottom of the plane, and the windows were still intact. Most of the ceiling was torn off during the crash, but one of the overhead bins remained above them.

The lid of the bin and the seats had melted. The fire charred everything, burning the steel into a black crisp. The fire originated from the front row as well as part of the exterior, so the flames were slowly being extinguished by the mud as the wreckage sank. The fire spread to some of the neighboring vines and branches, though.

One passenger sat in the front row in the aisle seat, legs buried in mud. Another passenger sat in the second row in the window seat. The row in the back was empty—but there were no empty seats before their departure from the Los Angeles International Airport. The passengers in that third row were plucked from their chairs mid-air and hurled into the jungle.

The front passenger was decapitated. His head was nowhere to be found, so it was safe to assume he was decapitated before landing in the bog.

The fire burned the clothing and skin off his body. His muscles turned black. White, red, and yellow were visible under and around the charred muscles. His intestines and other organs appeared to be falling out of his abdomen—yellow and red, wet and slimy. The yellow parts might have been fat and the white parts could have been pieces of bone, but it was too difficult to confirm.

If she didn't die during the crash, if she survived

for even a *minute* after landing in the jungle, the second passenger suffered from a more horrific death.

The woman's burnt fingers were wrapped around her seatbelt. The skin of her index fingers and thumbs blackened and melted, dribbling *into* the steel buckle at the center. She struggled to remove the belt at some point during the crash. Some of her burnt clothing remained on her body—tight jeans, a lightweight v-neck sweater.

Most of the visible parts of her skin were scorched by the fire—her hands, her collarbone, her neck, her face. Nearly ninety-percent of her scalp was burned off her head, leaving only small patches of frizzy blonde hair protruding from her skull. Her face was a mixture of blacks, whites, and reds. She sat with her mouth agape, but her tongue was pushed back *into* her throat and her teeth were falling out of her gums.

Her eyeballs had melted because of the extreme heat produced by the fire, the gooey vitreous fluid rolling down her cheeks—*hanging* from her face like hot cheese on a slice of pizza.

Nathan held his hand over his mouth and gagged. He didn't have to bite or lick the burnt bodies. The smell alone allowed him to taste death. And it was a flavor—a *powerful* tang—he would never forget. He leaned forward and vomited. The brown puke landed on his boots.

Cole stood in front of him and blocked his view of the carnage. He patted Nathan's back and said, "Don't look. You don't have to look at this. Come on, let it all out. Take your time."

Nathan coughed up a blob of foamy saliva. He kept retching and gagging, but he couldn't vomit again. He lost his lunch during the crash after all, but he just couldn't stop his natural reaction to stress and dread. After five minutes of sobbing and coughing, he composed himself. Tears cleaned his sooty cheeks, drool hung from his mouth.

"You good?" Cole asked. Nathan responded with a nod, although he shook and whimpered. Cole said, "Good, good. Now I know you're not going to want to hear this, but... I'm going to need you to get closer to those seats."

"What? *Why?* No, I can't. I can't do that, Cole. They're–"

"*Because*," Cole interrupted, his voice stern but understanding. Nathan closed his mouth and breathed through his nose, fighting the urge to kick and scream. Cole explained, "Because you can move, Nathan. Your ankles, your legs... You can walk around that mud and reach the overhead bin without a single problem. You see that log right there? Just stand on it, look through their carry-on bags, then come back with any useful supplies."

"But they–they're dead. They're really dead..."

"I know, I know. I'd do it on my own if I could, but it's impossible. If I get stuck in that mud 'cause of my busted ankle, then I'm either trapped or dead. If that happens, then you'd be on your own. But you can do this, Nathan. Just don't look at them, okay? Look anywhere but there. Help me. Help *us* survive this. Please."

Nathan let out a shaky sigh. He knew Cole was correct with his assessment. He needed courage in order to survive. *Man up,* he told himself, *if you ever want to see your family again, you have to do this.* He stepped forward. He heard every grain of dirt *crunching* under his boot. He took another step towards the cabin. He glanced up at the sky, hoping to hear the sound of a rescue chopper.

He only heard his painful, whistling breaths, the sound of his footsteps, and the roar of a fire. Cole's rambling and the sounds of nature were muffled, as if he were swimming underwater.

He stood up on the log, his eyes on the overhead locker. He saw the charred bodies in his peripheral vision. The corpses became a blur as tears filled his eyes. For the first time since the crash, he was happy to cry. His tears protected him, his tears strengthened him.

He reached into the overhead bin and pulled out a duffel bag. He found some extra clothes, grooming products, and a passport. He told himself not to do it, but he couldn't resist. He opened the passport and frowned.

He muttered, "Twenty-one years old... God, you were just a kid."

He put the passport in his back pocket in hopes of bringing some closure to the victim's friends and family. He grabbed a large purse from the overhead bin. He found a scarf, a wallet, another passport, and some make-up. He also found a half-empty water bottle.

He looked at the passport and whispered, "Thirty-six. My age. Did you... Did you have kids? Were you married? Were you single? Were you lonely? Hmm?

Did you die alone or did you leave a family behind? God, it's awful either way, isn't it? I'm so sorry." He slipped the passport into his back pocket and hopped off the log. He approached Cole and said, "I could only find this water bottle and some passports and some clothes. Nothing useful."

"Keep the water," Cole responded. "We need as much as that as we can get. Remember: every drop counts."

He looked through a luggage case a few meters away from the wreckage. He tossed a large pea coat over his shoulder and then a blazer over the other.

"Shit," he muttered. He closed the luggage, then he hobbled his way back to Nathan. He said, "The weather is good, it's warm and sunny, but we never know when we'll need protection. These coats should help us stay dry when it rains. We could use some more water, but we have enough for now, I think. Hell, we could even drink rainwater if another storm comes around. We don't need food yet, so... so we should focus on building shelter. We can build something with branches and leaves. We could even use some of the clothes in the luggage. Yeah, yeah, that can work..."

He gazed into Nathan's eyes, but he noticed Nathan wasn't paying attention. He looked off in the distance, eyes as hollow as a meth addict's. He looked over his shoulder and peered into the woods, searching for whatever had struck fear into his fellow survivor's heart. Then he saw it. He closed his eyes within a second of seeing it, but the image already carved itself into his mind.

About thirty meters away from the crash site,

surrounded by leaves and vines, a beam of sunshine penetrated the trees and dawned on a small body slumped up against a tree trunk. The body, covered in soot, couldn't have been larger than four and a half feet tall. Her blonde pigtails—which were partially black due to the fires on the plane—glowed with the sunshine.

From their angle, the men could clearly see the girl's face was *smashed* against the tree. If they moved her body, they knew they'd discover a faceless girl. They'd only see blood, brains, and bone.

Cole stumbled forward, threw his arm around Nathan, and then he spun him around. Nathan shambled ahead, his face pale and his eyes dim. The men walked away from the wreckage and the dead child.

Cole said, "I'm sorry you had to see that. It's not something anyone should experience. That chi-" He choked up before he could finish the word—*child, that child, that dead child.* He said, "It's horrible. That's all I can really say about it. This was a tragedy."

His head down, eyes on the rough terrain below him, Nathan sniffled and said, "We really are the 'lucky' ones, huh?"

Chapter Four

Strength in Numbers

"Monica!" a woman's trembling voice echoed through the jungle. "Monica, please answer me! Monica!"

Nathan and Cole sat on a pair of large stones protruding from the ground. Nathan held a water bottle up to his mouth, but he didn't take another swig. Cole stared into the trees in front of him. The men turned their heads slowly until they made eye contact. With their big, bugged-out eyes, they shared the same reaction: *holy shit.*

Before they could say a word, a man shouted, "Jennifer! Jennifer, honey, we're here! Follow my voice!"

"Mommy!" a boy screamed, his voice raspy from his excessive yelling and sobbing.

Nathan stared down at his hands as he tried to close the bottle. Yet again, he couldn't stop himself from shaking. For a moment, the sound of the water *slushing* in the bottle blocked out everything else. Anxiety, fear, and excitement blended in his body. He feared the worst: *dangerous survivors.* But he hoped for the best: *the rescue team.*

He looked at Cole and stuttered, "Re–Rescue?"

Cole said, "No, no, it can't be. A rescue team wouldn't sound like that. They wouldn't sound like they just lost everything in the world, they wouldn't sound like us. There's desperation in their voices. Can't you hear it?"

The woman yelled, "Monica! God, where are you?!"

Cole said, "They're survivors."

"And they're getting closer," Nathan responded as he looked out into the trees.

The men moved into the jungle, Cole dragging his injured leg behind him and Nathan gripping the chest of his shirt as he struggled to breathe. They stumbled past bushes and slid down short hills. They avoided a nine-foot bushmaster snake, taking a detour around a set of thick trees. They wanted to reach the other survivors as soon as possible, but they weren't willing to tangle with a snake. Nathan nearly fainted just by catching a glimpse of it.

"Hey!" Cole shouted as he hopped forward. He tripped on a root, but he caught himself on a tree. He leaned against the trunk and yelled, "Hey! Back here!"

The woman turned around quickly, her arm cocked back with a heavy stone in her hand—she was ready to pitch it at anyone or anything. She carried a large backpack and a duffel bag. A man stood beside her, his chiseled face covered in stubble and his graying hair matted with clumps of dirt. He carried a nine-year-old boy on his back. The boy's bowl cut was disheveled, his face and arms bruised, and his left leg splinted with a tent pole and a stick. All of their clothing was torn and disarranged.

Nathan jogged to Cole's side. He raised his hands up, as if to say: *wait, we come in peace.* The woman's brown, teary eyes darted between them. After surviving such a harrowing experience, she didn't know who to trust or what to expect. The man sat the boy down beside a tree, he coddled him when he mewled in pain, and then he turned his attention to

Nathan and Cole—*his fists clenched*. Like the woman, he was ready to fight. The boy sat there and shivered, traumatized.

Cole explained, "Let's calm down here. We–We're not going to hurt you, okay? You were on the plane, right? We were there, too. We, um, landed a few miles that way. We've been looking for supplies and people and... and rescue. That's all."

The man, the woman, and the boy analyzed the men from head-to-toe. Before they got a good look at them, they looked like shadows. And shadows looked like death. The man and woman whispered at each other without taking their eyes off Nathan and Cole. They nodded in agreement.

The woman lowered the stone and stepped forward. She said, "I'm sorry about that. We're just scared, you know? We don't... I don't... This is all just so fucked up. We're just looking for our friends and families. We didn't know you were on the–the pla–plane. We did–didn't know there were really others like us out here. We didn't..."

She covered her face with both hands and wept. She was still struggling to process the situation. She survived what should have been a non-survivable plane crash after all. The woman was also young. Her reactions were understandable. They gave her a minute to vent and cry.

Cole said, "It's okay, it's alright. We're all part of a miracle. This was a tragedy, but, just like I told my friend here, we're alive. We owe it to the victims to survive. We can do that together, okay?" He pointed at Nathan and said, "This is Nathan and my name is

Cole. What are your names? Come on, let's get friendly."

Wiping the tears from her cheeks, Mariah said, "My name is Mariah. Mariah Henderson."

"The name's Michael Watson," the other man said, his voice confident and stern.

"I–I'm Dylan," the boy squeaked out from the ground.

"My son. That crash really banged him up, so I'd appreciate it if you kept an eye on him. That's *if* we're going to survive this thing together."

Nathan stepped forward and asked, "Why were you like that?"

"What do you mean 'why?' I don't know how he broke his leg, but I know–"

"No, no, not you," Nathan interrupted. He looked at Mariah and said, "You. Why were you ready to attack us like that? What got you worked up? Did you... Did you see something out here?"

Mariah nodded. Nathan felt the lump in his throat growing. His overactive imagination sent horrific ideas through his mind. He remembered the graphic horror films he watched as a child.

"I saw a snake," Mariah said. "A *big* fucking snake."

Nathan responded, "Snakes are better than zombies and cannibals, but... I'll be honest: I'm scared shitless of snakes, too. Some snakes can kill us with one bite."

"Zombies? *Zombies?*" Michael repeated, his hands on his hips. He said, "I don't have time for this shit. We can survive together, sure, but I'm not going to stand around here and protect you from snakes and goddamn zombies!"

Cole responded, "No one's asking you to protect us from anything."

"Good. My wife, Jennifer, is missing. We got separated during the crash. I have to find her so please get out of my way."

Cole hopped in front of him on one foot and blocked his path. He said, "We should stick together. There's strength in numbers."

"Strength? Look at your leg. You're useless. Now listen to me: I *need* to find my wife."

Cole wanted to ask: *when was the last time you saw her? Are you sure she's still alive?* He believed his questions were valid. They couldn't run around the jungle searching for one dead body. But he wasn't heartless. He couldn't challenge Michael, especially with Dylan nearby.

He looked at Dylan's leg and said, "If we're discussing injuries, then I'm about as useful as your son."

Glaring at him, Michael said, "What did you just–"

"I'm not trying to fight you," Cole interrupted. He chuckled, then he said, "I'd clearly lose that fight. I only want you to think about your next decision. Your son is injured, but he's safe with you. You know where he is, he knows where you are. You know his condition, he knows... Well, you get what I'm saying. You should think about what's certain before you go barreling head-first into uncharted territory. I'm assuming you haven't vacationed here before, right?"

Michael unclenched his fists and stepped back. Cole saw the rage and pain in his eyes. He was a family man who wanted to save his family. Dylan watched as a group of spider monkeys swung on the branches above them. Mariah leaned against a tree and watched the men. She had been searching for her friend, Monica, in the jungle as well. Cole's warning brought her back to reality. Self-preservation was the only thing on her mind.

Nathan handed Michael the water bottle and said, "Take a drink. We'll keep looking for some water and supplies. While we do that, you can search for your wife. We'll help as much as possible. Alright?"

Michael responded, "Yeah, alright. But just because I'm sticking with you that doesn't mean I'm going to stop looking for her."

"I would never ask you to stop. I know family is important. Believe me, I know..."

Cole said, "I'll help you as soon as my leg gets better. I promise, we'll find your loved ones and we *will* get out of this alive. We can do this, guys." He limped forward and said, "But we're going to have to move. We saw a big snake back there and I don't think we want to set up camp near that thing. Do you?"

Mariah said, "Hell no. Let's go."

***

The sun fell behind the trees, painting the sky with broad strokes of yellow, orange, and red. During the day, Nathan and Michael scavenged the nearby wreckage while Cole and Mariah built their shelter near some trees and a pond. Dylan wanted to help, he begged and he whined, but he couldn't do much due to his broken leg. So, he sat and watched from the shade of a tree.

Nathan and Michael stumbled upon some burnt corpses during their search. Although he had already witnessed the mayhem first-hand, Nathan couldn't look at the bodies without gagging or retching or crying. Michael was disturbed by the death, he wasn't apathetic, but he had to examine every corpse thoroughly. *Jennifer*—he had to know if she survived the crash.

Meanwhile, Cole and Mariah built tents out of tree saplings, palm leaves, and some coats and blankets. A powerful gust of wind could have blown the makeshift tents down, but it was the best they could do without the proper supplies. When Nathan and Michael returned, they built a campfire and lit it using a lighter, plants, twigs, and Michael's tie.

"Dad," Dylan said, a cup of fruit—one of the last from the plane's galley—in his hand. "Where's mommy? Did she call you yet?"

Michael opened his mouth to speak, but he couldn't say a word. He saw the innocence in his son's eyes. He couldn't lie to his face, so he looked away.

He said, "She, uh… She called and she… she said she was safe and that she loves us, she loves you, and she can't wait to see us when we meet up in a few days." Tears dripped from his eyes as he blinked. He pointed up at the sky and said, "She said to listen for the helicopters. They're on their way and they're going to get us out of here. Yeah, that's what she said."

Dylan heard the pain in his father's voice and he caught a glimpse of his tears, but he didn't know how to react. He sniffled and ate his fruit as he thought about his parents.

Trying to break the ice, Cole asked, "So, Mariah, where were you headed? If you don't mind me asking.

I mean, I'm not trying to–"

"I was going to Uruguay," Mariah responded, staring absently at the fire. "I just graduated from college last semester. I'm getting my... I *earned* my bachelor's in elementary education. I was going to be an elementary school teacher, you know? *We* were going to be teachers, my friends and me. We were coming to Uruguay just to travel, to explore, to party. One last adventure together..."

She laughed, but she wasn't happy. She couldn't control her nervous laughter. It was a natural reaction to the situation. Her smile twisted into a frown, her lips shaking uncontrollably.

"I missed my flight. Monica and I, we missed our first flight. All of our other friends are probably at the hotel right now—sad, scared, *devastated.* But, when I look at the bright side, I think: at least they're safe right now. I want to feel the same way about Monica. I want to find her and I want to leave this place with her. I *can't* go home without her. I *can't* face her family on my own. I can't, I just can't..."

Nathan wanted to cry with her. He wanted to talk about Holly and Kyle. The personal conversations only caused them more pain. *We'll have to talk about the crash someday, about the people we lost,* he thought, *but let's not make it today.* He handed Mariah a bag of peanuts and a water bottle. He nodded at her and communicated with his eyes. And Mariah understood him. She looked at Dylan, then at Michael, and then at Nathan. Her eyes said something along the lines of: *okay, I'll try to be strong.*

Nathan asked, "Dylan, what do you want to eat when you get home? Pizza? Ice cream? Or maybe a scoop of vanilla ice cream on top of a slice of pepperoni pizza?"

Ew!—Dylan exclaimed, grinning.

"What? You don't like pizza ice cream?"

"No! That's nasty!"

"Have you tried it before?"

"Nope, never."

"Then how do you know it's nasty?"

While Nathan and Dylan discussed their favorite foods, Cole beckoned to Michael and said, "Walk with me."

The men moved away from their campsite. They looked for more supplies nearby, opening every piece of luggage they stumbled upon.

As they walked, Cole considered telling Michael the hard truth: *your wife is dead.* He thought it would benefit their survival and Michael's mental health if he accepted the truth before doubt poisoned his mind. But, at heart, he was an unrelenting optimist. They survived a plane crash, so there *could* have been more survivors out there. And Jennifer, Michael's wife, could have been one of them. He decided to bite his tongue.

He asked, "Do you want to talk?"

"About what?" Michael responded.

"Anything."

"If you have something to say, say it. I'm an adult, I can handle it."

Cole's silence spoke for him.

Michael opened a bag in a bush and looked through the supplies. He said, "We were going to a wedding. I was going to be a groomsman. My old buddy was finally tying the knot, you know? Well, I'm guessing he still is. I hope he's not trying to reschedule the wedding because of all of this."

"He wasn't on the plane?"

"No, no. He moved to Uruguay a few years ago to pursue some business opportunities and he stayed after he met a beautiful, gentle Uruguayan woman. That woman became his best friend, just like Jennifer was... just like Jennifer *is* my best friend. I hope they'll have a healthy marriage, like my wife and I. Yeah, I wish them the best."

Cole said, "I can tell you're a good man, Michael. I wish good people like you, like your family, like Nathan, like Mariah... I wish none of us had to go through this. It might not mean much coming from a stranger, but I'm going to do my best to help you. I want us to survive this 'event' together. That includes Jennifer."

Michael stopped looking through the bag. He looked Cole in the eye. A spark of sincerity twinkled in his pupil. He hugged Cole and sobbed into his shoulder. He mumbled about the tragedy: *why did this have to happen to us? It's not fair. Jennifer doesn't deserve this. Dylan did nothing wrong.* He spent five minutes unleashing all of his emotional pain and anger.

He leaned away from Cole and said, "I'm sorry. I'm so sorry."

"You don't owe me or anyone else an apology. We're in this together, so we'll get out of this together. I'm giving you my word."

"Thank you. I'll do whatever I can to help, I promise."

"That's all we need."

They returned to the campsite. Cole sat down beside Nathan while Michael comforted his son. They ate two burritos, which were found under a seat in the jungle. Night crept up on them, accompanied by a soft, warm drizzle. The clouds obscured the stars and the rain extinguished the fire, leaving them in near pitch-black darkness.

Mariah asked, "Should someone stay awake? You know, to keep a lookout?"

"What?" Nathan responded, his brow furrowed. "Why do we need a lookout?"

"Big fuckin' snakes."

Cole said, "That might not be the only thing we have to worry about out here."

Don't say spiders, please don't say spiders, Nathan thought.

Cole explained, "I don't know everything, but I'm guessing we landed in Brazil. Maybe somewhere near the border with Peru. Either way, we're in the Amazon rainforest right now. There are a lot of dangerous animals and insects out here, sure, but there are also people. I'm talking… indigenous people, uncontacted tribes. Now think about it. We made one hell of an entrance, didn't we? We blew up in the sky and fell into their territory. We turned lightning and thunder into explosions, we turned regular rain into fire and blood. I wouldn't blame these people for thinking we might be invaders. It wouldn't be the first time their land was invaded and destroyed by foreign forces, right? So, we don't know what they'll do to us if they find us. That's all I'm saying."

The group sat in silence, only the soothing pitter-patter of raindrops hitting leaves and branches dancing through the jungle.

Michael said, "You guys get some sleep. I'll keep a lookout. I'm not tired anyway, and I might be the healthiest out of all of us."

"Can I stay up with you, daddy?" Dylan asked, eyes like a kitten's.

"That's not a good idea. You need sleep if you want your leg to get better."

"It's better, I swear!"

"I know it still hurts, Dylan. I need you to sleep. Don't worry, I'll wake you when I hear the helicopters."

Dylan pouted, then he nodded in agreement. Mariah beckoned to him. She allowed him to sleep in her tent. She offered him some sisterly protection. Nathan and Cole squeezed themselves into the other tents. Michael sat on a large stone near the edge of the pond. He stared into the dark jungle, but, for the first time since the crash, he didn't think about his wife.

He thought about the uncontacted people in the rainforest.

Chapter Five

In the Woods

"Mo–Mommy," Dylan mumbled, half-asleep.

He sat up, yawned, and stretched. He smacked his lips, his head bobbing as he drifted in-and-out of sleep. Then his eyes widened as he heard a snapping twig and a rapid succession of footsteps. He looked to his right. Mariah slept in the fetal position, her feet sticking out from under a large pea coat. Trails of fresh tears formed on her rosy, muddy cheeks. She couldn't stop crying, even while she slept.

Dylan reached for her, but, before he could touch her shoulder, he heard a soft voice outside of his tent. It sounded like a woman, but he couldn't understand her.

"*Mommy,*" he repeated with a hint of confidence in his voice.

He hissed in pain as he crawled out of the tent, dragging his injured leg across the mud. He felt like his shin was burning from within his limb. On his stomach, he stopped outside of his tent and looked around, ensuring everything was the same. Nathan and Cole slept in their tents—*check.* His father moved from the stone and fell asleep against a tree, but he was accounted for—*check.*

He stared into the jungle behind the tents. A few beams of moonlight penetrated the clouds and the branches, illuminating thin slits of the jungle—like sunshine entering a living room through a set of blinds. He heard the branches groaning and leaves rustling. He saw some shadowy figures in the trees, too. *Monkeys,* he thought. He didn't hear the voice again.

He crawled to his father's side, a grimace of pain on his face. He took the cell phone out of his hands. The battery had drained down to fifteen percent. He smiled as he unlocked the phone. He knew the passcode: *0615.* It represented his birthday, June 15th. He remembered sneaking the phone out of his dad's pockets to play video games back in their Los Angeles home.

His happiness was short-lived. On the screen, he saw an image of himself, his father, and his mother at a park—a family portrait. His father dozed off while looking at a picture of their family. The boy felt ill when he looked at his mother. He felt nauseous, lightheaded, and confused. It was as if he were staring at the picture of a deceased loved one. It was grief in its purest form.

But he was young, so he didn't understand it.

He panted and trembled and groaned. Just as he opened his mouth to scream, he heard another *cracking* twig behind him. Mouth ajar, he glanced over his shoulder. The silhouette of a person stood out against the moonlight. The large, bulky person stood behind Michael, his legs obscured by a bush. He appeared to be holding a large pole—*a spear?*

The man dashed away from the bush and ran deeper into the jungle. In less than five seconds, he was swallowed by the darkness and the sound of his footsteps was softened by the groaning branches until he couldn't be heard anymore. He was fast, and he ran without a limp or without hunching down.

Dylan gasped as he heard another set of footsteps from the other side of the pond. He saw several shadowy figures running through the jungle. He looked up at the trees and watched as the branches swayed and bounced, like coils of galvanized springs. He spotted the shadow of a person jumping from one branch to another.

"Not monkeys, not monkeys," he whispered as his voice trembled with fear. He scrambled to his father's side, forgetting the pain emanating from his leg. He shook his dad's shoulder and yelled, "Not monkeys! Dad, they're not monkeys! Daddy, please wake up! Please, please, please!"

Michael gasped as he awoke, slipping and sliding on the mud underneath him. He looked at his son with a set of wide, bulging eyes. The type of look that said: *what the hell are you talking about? And where am I?* Monkeys, monkeys, monkeys—at the very least, he understood his son was talking about monkeys. He saw several monkeys in the jungle already, so he wasn't surprised.

He looked up at the trees and stuttered, "Wha– What? What's going on, Dylan?"

"I saw something in the trees! Over there, in the trees! They weren't monkeys, daddy! I swear, they weren't monkeys!"

"Dylan, *relax.* Calm down, you're going to hurt yourself panicking like that."

"But I saw monsters! They were watching us!"

Cole limped out of his tent with a homemade torch. A bundle of torn clothing soaked in tree sap was tied to one end of the branch. He lit that end with a lighter and quickly illuminated their campsite. He heard everything—monkeys and monsters—while he struggled to escape his tent. He swung the torch in every direction as he teetered around their campsite.

Nathan and Mariah joined them, drowsy but curious. They didn't see anyone in the jungle. They didn't even see a single animal—no monkeys, no sloths, no snakes, no insects.

Teary-eyed, Dylan said, "I saw something. I really did. I'm not lying. I think, um... They, um..." He wanted to explain himself, but the image of the man with the pole frightened him. He said, "I think they wanna hurt me."

Michael responded, "No one wants to hurt you. You were just having a bad dream."

"But I'm awake!"

"I know, I know. It's just a... I don't know how to explain it to you, but it wasn't real, okay? It's just part of your imagination. If there are people out there, they wouldn't run from us. The only people out here are us, other survivors like your mother, and the rescue team that's looking for us. Do you understand me?"

Dylan said, "I think... you're wrong. They–They're out there. They–"

He clenched his teeth, his face scrunched up into a bundle of ridges.

Michael asked, "What's wrong? Are you okay? Hey, talk to me, kiddo."

"My stomach. I feel... bad."

His entire body began to shake. A cold sweat glistened on his face and neck. He began swallowing his saliva as quickly as possible, but he couldn't fight it. He vomited the burrito, then he tottered around. Michael caught him before he could fall. He sat him down on his lap and placed the back of his hand on his forehead.

Mariah approached and said, "Here, let me check on him."

"Is he sick?" Michael asked. "Is it bad?"

Cole and Nathan checked the area. The thing about nature was: *it was alive.* From the wind to the animals, the trees and bushes to the ponds and rivers, everything made noise in the wilderness. It was normal.

Cole shouted, "Hello! Is anyone out there? We're survivors! We're not going to hurt you! Hello!"

Nathan's eyes darted to the right. Barely illuminated by Cole's torch, he saw a shadow dashing through the jungle from the corner of his eye. He examined the neighboring tree, watching the branches as they shook with the wind, then he looked at the shadow it cast. The branch's shadow didn't match the silhouette he spotted.

"Not monkeys?" he whispered in a doubtful tone. "Then what the hell is out here?"

Without looking back at him, Cole asked, "You see anything?" Nathan kept staring into the jungle, suspicion written on his face. Cole said, "Nathan, I need you to stay with me. Do you see anything?"

Yes, I saw something—Nathan couldn't admit it. If it was nothing, he didn't want to ignite Dylan's imagination with tales of shadowy monsters in the woods.

He stuttered, "N–No. I–I don't see anything. It's just us, I think."

Cole responded, "I don't see anything, either." He cupped his free hand around his mouth and shouted, "If you're out there, don't be afraid of us! We're like you! We're just people! We won't hurt you, okay? We're the good guys! We... We have water and food! And we need rescue!"

There was no response.

Mariah placed the back of her hand on Dylan's neck and then on his chest. His sweat was worrisome, but his fever was mild. Blood vessels spread across his eyes, like cracks on a window pane, but he stayed conscious and alert.

She said, "I don't think he's sick. Maybe he has a slight fever, but he looks fine. Well..."

"What? What do you think?" Michael asked. He shook his son gently and asked, "How are you feeling? What's wrong?"

Mariah said, "I think he's scared. I think he's more scared than usual. It's cliché, but he looks like he just saw a ghost. Maybe he did see something out here."

The group became silent. They glanced around as they thought about the many possibilities. They were adults, they could tell fiction from reality, but the same idea crept into all of their heads: *monsters.* The boogeyman—a monster they each defeated as children—snuck out from under the bed and waited for them in the jungle, as if the imaginary creature had predicted the crash.

Cole said, "You should all get some rest. I'll stay up and keep a lookout. Michael, take my tent and take care of your kid."

Michael carried his son to one of the makeshift tents. He tried to comfort him by telling him a story about talking trees and curious monkeys. Mariah nodded and waved at Cole and Nathan. She would have offered to stay awake throughout the night, but she couldn't muster the courage or the energy. The tragedy rendered her lethargic. She returned to her tent and threw the pea coat over her body.

Nathan took the torch from Cole and said, "I should stay up, not you. Your leg is still busted, Cole. You need rest more than I do."

"I don't know about that. How's your chest?"

"It still hurts when I breathe, but it's not so bad anymore. Or maybe I'm just getting used to it. Either way, I'm fine. I can stay awake. Get some sleep. I'll wake you at sunrise or if I see anything suspicious."

"Alright, alright. Thanks, man. I appreciate it."

Nathan lit the campfire with the torch, but he didn't extinguish the torch afterward. The light brought a sense of security to his mind. He sat down across from the tents at an angle, so he could watch his fellow survivors and the jungle to his left. He gazed into the darkness beyond his light and wondered what hid from them in the woods—or what was watching them from the trees.

Chapter Six

The Discovery

Less than a quarter mile away from their camp, Mariah stumbled upon a strip of flatland beside a creek. The water appeared green due to the reflecting vegetation and the morning sunshine, but it was tantalizing. A capybara drank water from the other side of the stream. The large rodent ignored the fish, and vice versa.

She couldn't take the risk, though. If the water were contaminated, she didn't want to contract any diseases by drinking it. She knew about the piranhas swimming in the rivers and lakes of the rainforest, too.

Without looking back, she shouted, "This looks like a good place!"

Nathan and Cole emerged from the jungle behind her. Michael followed them, carrying Dylan on his back.

Mariah said, "There aren't as many trees and it's next to water, so it should be visible from the sky. I say we make our signal right here."

Cole asked, "What's the plan?"

"Well, we grab some stones and create a large SOS signal along the river. Maybe two, maybe three, or maybe we just won't stop until we're out of rocks or they find us."

"We can start a fire, too," Nathan suggested. "A big one, you know?"

Michael placed Dylan down beside a tree. He said, "You stay here and help the nice lady. She needs rocks, okay? Toss some her way and stay away from any animals you see. I'm going to try to call your mother again." As he walked into the jungle, he shouted, "Cole, please keep an eye on him! I'll be right back!"

"Alright! Don't stray too far," Cole shouted. He looked at Nathan and said, "We can start small, controlled fires, but I don't think it would be wise of us to start a big one."

"Why not?"

"We crash landed here, man. How many fires has this crash started already? How many acres have we burned? Even if it's not our fault, huh? Sure, the rain can put some of those fires out, but what if we start one that the rain can't stop? What if it roars out of control, corners us, and burns us to death? I'm not a fire expert, so I don't think we should take that risk."

Nathan responded, "But that's the problem. There are so many burning pieces of wreckage out here already. How will they know where to start searching?"

As she placed rocks down beside the creek, slowly forming a giant 'S,' Mariah said, "That's what the signal is for. If we find a few flares, then they can't miss us."

Nathan said, "Flares... That can work, but..." He sighed in frustration and stared up at the clear sky. He said, "God, I just don't understand. I haven't heard a single jet or helicopter or anything since the crash. We're talking about an airplane from a commercial airline, guys. There were hundreds of us in there so hundreds of people are dead. You'd think they'd be rushing in here to save us."

Cole said, "I don't get it, either. There has to be some sort of problem out here. Maybe they really lost track of us, maybe it's the weather, maybe it's political, maybe it's something else..."

Michael lunged through the dense bushes and foliage. He peeked over his shoulder every ten steps, afraid he might lose his way in the rainforest. He looked at his cell phone—six-percent battery life remaining. He couldn't find any signal in the wilderness.

He shouted, "Jennifer! Jennifer, if you're stuck, if you can hear me, give me a sign! I'm here, honey! I'm here and Dylan is okay! Jennifer!" He heard a rustling bush to his left. Wide-eyed, he rushed towards the bush and yelled, "Honey! Sweetie! I'm coming! Oh God, don't move!"

He crashed into the bush, twigs snapping and leaves falling, and slid to a stop before completely bulldozing through it. He watched as a small monkey ran off and climbed a nearby tree. He stared at the muddy ground, disappointment shattering his heart. Jennifer was nowhere in sight. He fell to his knees and whimpered.

He mumbled, "Jen–Jennifer, I'm sorry. I can't feel you anymore. I don't know if–if you're alive or–or... or dead. This is my fault. I shouldn't have asked you and Dylan to come with me. I shouldn't have accepted his request. We were so happy at home. Everything was going so well. What have I done? Why did this have to happen to us? What did we do, goddammit?!" His face went from pale to rosy within seconds. A drop of saliva hanging from his chapped lip, he looked up at the trees and whispered, "God, if you won't save us, *all* of us, why don't you just get it over with and kill us already?"

He heard another snapping twig behind him. He struggled to his feet and looked back. He saw trees, bushes, vines, foliage, and mud—but he didn't see any animals.

He asked, "Is someone there?"

The jungle was eerily silent.

He wiped the tears off his face and stepped forward. He walked with his shoulders raised and eyes narrowed, scared but curious. He pushed past the bushes and vines—five meters, fifteen meters, *thirty meters*. He heard the sound of buzzing flies. He saw them soaring around each other a few meters ahead, dozens of black specks in his vision.

"What the hell?" he muttered. "Jennifer, is that you?"

As he approached the flies, he caught a whiff of a vile scent. A sulfurous, gassy, rotten stench stained the area, ingrained into the mud, the leaves, and the wood. He recognized it as the scent of death, but he couldn't stop moving forward. He needed to check every deceased corpse in order to confirm his wife's condition.

He said, "Please, don't let it be you. I'm begging you, don't let it–"

He lost his footing as he stepped past a bush. He rolled down a short two-meter hill and ended up on his back. He found himself staring up at the trees again.

He asked, "Is this the best you've got for me? You

really think you can kill me like this? You can do better, can't you? You..."

He stopped, squinted again, and tilted his head to the side. He noticed the flies buzzing over him. Some of the flies landed on his arms and face. He saw the hill to his left and another hill down by his feet. *No, not hills,* he thought. He was in a ditch, so one question ran through his mind: *why would there be a ditch large enough to fit a human body in the middle of the jungle?*

Then he felt it. He felt the ridges and the edges underneath him, poking his back. He glanced over his shoulder. For a moment, he didn't hear anything in the jungle. The world was muted, moving in slow motion around him. After ten seconds, everything came back, and he realized he was shrieking at the top of his lungs.

Nathan and Cole stopped discussing their options, Mariah and Dylan dropped their rocks. Cole limped into the jungle and followed Michael's screech. Nathan followed him, but then he stopped in his tracks upon hearing Mariah's footsteps.

He said, "Wait. You have to stay here."

"What? Why?"

"Just trust me."

"What if he needs help? I'm not a doctor, but I know a thing or two about first-aid."

Nathan shook his head and, in a hushed voice, he said, "Stay with the kid. What if it's... 'her?' He shouldn't see her like that. Just wait here, okay? Protect him. Please."

Mariah nodded and said, "Okay, okay. You're right."

She hugged Dylan and said, "Don't worry. Your dad probably found a snake out there. He knows how to take care of himself. Come on, cutie, help me finish this signal."

Dylan had a thousand questions: *where's my dad? Why is he screaming? Is he hurt? Is it because of my mom?* But he didn't get a single answer from her.

Nathan ran into the jungle. He saw Michael leaning against a tree, gagging and sobbing. Cole wobbled, as if he were about to collapse, his crutch on the ground beside him. Their skin whitened, their eyes reddened, their hair prickled. Nathan stopped between them. His eyes widened and his mouth fell open as he stared down the short hill. It took less than five seconds before the color faded from his lips. He resembled his fellow survivors—a wobbly stone sculpture.

It wasn't a ditch. *It was a grave.*

Two nude bodies rested at the bottom, face-down. Covered in mud, their skin became gray. Some of their veins thickened, purple and blue and even black. Stab wounds riddled their bodies—from their shoulders down to the small of their backs, and from their asses to their calves. The blood around their wounds was fresh, but it had started drying, blackening and hardening.

Nathan stuttered, "Th–This... Wha–What is this? How did... What the hell are we looking at?" He dug his fingers into his hair and cried, saliva spurting from his mouth. He shouted, "Fuck! What the hell is this?! What are we going to do?!"

"Try to keep your voice down," Cole said. "I don't want the boy to hear about this."

"The boy? Cole, the–there are two de–de... dead people in front of us. They look like... like they were slaughtered. Oh, shit, what do we do?"

"I think the first thing we should do is, well, find the cause of death. In order to do that, one of us will have to... flip them over so we can assess the damage."

"Are you serious?"

Cole responded, "I wish I wasn't. I don't think they died during the crash. No, these wounds weren't 'accidental.' They're fresher, more *brutal* than that. These people were killed just a few hours ago. What if they survived like us and they were killed by something out here? Like a jaguar? An anaconda? A mad ape? A... A person? Do you want to be out here knowing someone or something is watching us at night? Stalking us, *hunting us?*"

Nathan kept his eyes on Cole, waiting for him to crack a smile or snicker—*just kidding.* But he was dead serious.

Michael said, "I'm sorry, but I can't go back down there. I thought I could, but I can't. I'm weak, I'm fucking pathetic. If it's my wife down there, I can–can't... I can't... I can't look. Please, don't make me."

"I can't, either," Cole said, his somber eyes on the bodies. "My leg is just too messed up for me to crawl down there, flip 'em over, climb out... I'm sorry."

Why are you apologizing?—Nathan thought about asking the question, but he already knew the answer. Michael was traumatized by the discovery, and Cole couldn't physically handle the job. He pushed his sleeves up and stepped up to the edge. The flies landed on his hair, face, and arms, but they didn't bother him. The dead bodies terrified him so much that his other senses were briefly deactivated.

He took a deep breath, ignoring the pain in his chest, then he slid down into the grave. He fell to his knees near the corpses, his hands leveled with his shoulders and his palms facing downward, like a puppet master pulling some strings. He hesitated, he didn't know where to start, but he knew he had to do something. *Cole's right,* he thought, *what if something's really trying to kill us out here?*

He frowned as he grabbed the body, one hand on an arm and the other on a thigh. The limbs were cold and stiff. He flipped the body over. Twigs, leaves, and dirt spiraled into the air in front of him.

"Jesus Christ," he muttered as he leaned back against the hill.

The first victim was a young male—perhaps in his late twenties. His face was beaten until every inch of his skin turned into a shade of purple. Blood bubbled out of the massive knots on his face. His eyes weren't visible from any angle. There were small bite marks across his forearms and hands, as if someone were nibbling on him. Like his back, his torso and thighs were stabbed repeatedly, but his arteries were spared—*on purpose.* Someone wanted him to suffer from a long, painful death.

His nipples were torn off his chest, leaving small, bloody craters on his firm pectoral muscles. Some of the skin around his areolas was also removed.

Although blood covered his crotch, from his waist to his thighs, the young man's mutilated genitals—or what was left of them—were clearly visible. His penis was sawed off at the base, leaving a dark red nub on his crotch. His scrotum was hacked open. One of his bloody testicles hung onto his scrotum by its spermatic cord. The other testicle was missing. They could see white, red, and even blue inside of his scrotum.

Projectile vomit nearly shot out of Nathan's mouth, but he sealed his lips, closed his eyes, and turned away. He choked the puke down as he breathed deeply through his nose. Tears oozed past his eyelids and flowed down his cheeks. The gore was horrific. It wasn't like the horror movies or the videos of murder people circulated online. It was real— bloody, disgusting, and *real.*

Michael vomited on his shoes while Cole leaned against the tree and wheezed. Death was always a difficult subject, but murder was different. It was unusual, jarring, and visceral. Most people didn't discover horrifically mutilated corpses during their lifetimes. And that man was, without a doubt, murdered.

Nathan stuttered, "Wh–Who would do some- something like this? They... Oh my God, they slaughtered him. This wasn't an animal. N–No way, no fucking way." He tried to slide up the hill with his back against the mud. He said, "I have to get out of this. I'm going to–to puke. I can't do this, I just can't."

"Don't quit," Cole said. Nathan stopped crawling. Cole coughed, then he said, "I know it's difficult, but you can't stop. We have to know what happened to the other... victim. We have to know if it's..."

Her—Nathan could hear the word without Cole

finishing his sentence. He glanced over at Michael and thought about the man's wife. An image of Holly and Kyle flashed in his mind. If he were in Michael's shoes, he would want closure, too. Although reluctant, he nodded at Cole and proceeded with the plan.

He tossed some leaves over the dead man's mutilated genitals. He reached over the man's body and grabbed the other corpse's shoulder and waist. He lifted the body from the ground and pushed until the corpse rolled over. He felt the warmth escape from his body in an instant, as if all of the blood were drained from his veins. A terrifying numbness set in.

This is what death feels like, he thought. *I am alive, but I am dead. I am on Earth, but I am walking through Hell.*

The woman's eyes were gouged out, leaving two black holes on her face. Ants marched in and out of her gaping mouth. Her tongue was severed while her teeth were either chipped or yanked out of her pulpy, bloody gums. At her waist, a long, wide cut stretched from one hip to the other. Through the cut, her abdomen was hollowed out. Her organs were missing—her stomach, her small and large intestines, her liver, her gallbladder, *everything.*

Like the male victim, her genitals weren't spared. Her crotch was smashed and crushed with a heavy stone. Her pelvic bones were shattered and pushed into her body, consequently crushing her uterus. She was penetrated with a sharp, spiky object. A piece of her vagina hung out of her body, a mushy blob between her thighs. She passed out during the genital mutilation, then she died during the disembowelment. The human body wasn't built to handle so much pain.

His teeth chattering, Michael stammered, "It–It–It's not her. It's not–not my Jennifer. Thank Go–"

He stopped himself from uttering those words— *thank God.* In the jungle, his wife missing and two mutilated bodies in a grave in front of him, he couldn't thank anyone for their current situation. The brutal reality of life quickly extinguished his spark of hope. The discovery introduced new threats to their fight for survival.

"I need to find her," Michael said in a low, awed voice. "If someone or something is killing people like... like *this,* then I need to find my wife. Just look at what they did to these people! Look at this! It's... It's not possible! This can't be real!"

Cheeks as red as apples, Cole responded, "It's real, and we have to face it."

Nathan crawled out of the grave, slowed by a sudden sense of lethargy. He walked past the men, ignoring their muffled voices. He stared down at his trembling hands, stained with fresh mud and dry blood. He wiped his hands on his pants. The mud slid off his palms in thick goops while the blood clung to his skin.

He asked, "What is happening? Why haven't I woken up yet?"

"This is real!" Cole snapped. He sighed, then he hobbled away from the grave. He said, "These people were murdered. Maybe they were passengers on our plane, maybe they're locals from the area. It doesn't matter, does it? Someone slaughtered them, and that person or those *people* are probably still out here. We need to do something about this."

Michael stepped forward, but he staggered after the first step. He was lightheaded due to the extreme violence. It took a mental toll on him.

He leaned against another tree and said, "Murdered... Wha–What can we do? Jennifer, she's still out there, so I'm not leaving. And you said you'd help me find her. So, what's the plan, Cole?"

"Well, we don't have a lot of options. The best thing we can do is... is move away from this—from them. Maybe, maybe... Okay, stay with me here. Maybe this was some type of tribal violence, right? There are uncontacted people out here, remember? These people could have been slaughtered during some type of war or something, right?"

"They didn't look like they belonged to a tribe," Nathan said with a monotonous voice, staring absently at his hands.

"Then maybe they were, you know, deforesters and they bumped heads with the wrong group. We don't have all of the details and we're not here to investigate. We only know that something tragic happened here. So, I say we grab all our supplies, we cross that river, and we start a new camp. Who knows? Maybe there are other survivors over there. What are you guys thinking? Hmm?"

"They looked like us," Nathan said as tears dripped onto his hands.

Swiping at his face, Michael walked ahead of them and stuttered, "I–I don't know what to do anymore. I only need to–to find Jennifer and, um... and I have to take care of Dylan. My son... He needs me."

Cole asked, "Nathan, will you be okay?" Nathan couldn't say a single word. Cole pushed him gently and said, "Let's get back to the others. Hey, don't let this break you. You hear me? Come on, let's go."

Nathan followed Cole's lead, shambling every step of the way. He kept staring at his hands. It was too late. His mind had already shattered, the chunks rattling in his skull like the pieces to a puzzle in an old cardboard box. He thought he saw the worst of humanity during the crash, but, at heart, he knew the worst was yet to come.

Chapter Seven

The Trees

Nathan, Cole, and Michael lumbered out of the jungle and returned to the creek. Within seconds, Mariah noticed their pale, sweaty skin, rosy noses, and bloodshot eyes.

She stood up and asked, "What's wrong? What happened out there?"

Cole groaned as he fell to his knees near the creek. He took a sip of water from his cupped hands, then he splashed it on his face. Nathan scrubbed his hands under the water. The mud chipped off his fingernails and followed the current, leaving trails of muddy water behind, but the blood remained. Michael knelt down and hugged his son, fighting the urge to cry as he breathed shakily and trembled.

Mariah asked, "Michael, are you okay? We heard screaming."

Leaning close to his son's ear, Michael kept repeating the same sentence: *your mother is okay, your mother is okay, your mother is okay.*

"Talk to me, Cole," Mariah said.

Cole approached the tree closest to Michael and Dylan. He leaned back against the tree and slid down to his ass. He was physically and mentally exhausted. He had already discussed the situation with Michael and Nathan, he didn't want to repeat himself for Mariah and Dylan. He didn't want to relive the awful moment.

The bodies. The dead, mutilated bodies.

Mariah crossed her arms, nodded at Nathan, and said, "I guess you're not going to say anything, either, right?"

And, just as she predicted, Nathan stood there and stared at her. He didn't want to talk about it and, even if he did, he didn't know where to begin.

Those bodies. Those dead, mutilated bodies.

Dylan asked, "What happened, dad? Why did you scream?"

"Don–Don't worry about that," Michael responded. "I just, um... How are you feeling? Huh? Are you feeling better?"

"I don't know. I feel sick again. It's my stomach. I don't know how to say it. Something's wrong with me."

"No. No, kiddo, nothing's wrong with you. It's just anxiety, okay? Fear and anxiety. It does that to people. I've felt it before."

"Do you feel it... now?"

Michael bit his lip and exhaled through his nose. *Yes*—the answer was obvious, even to his nine-year-old son. He felt anxious, scared, confused, and sick. His mind was crumbling due to the stress. He survived a crash and landed in the middle of a jungle, lost his wife, and stumbled upon two victims of murder.

Flustered, Mariah asked, "Is anyone going to tell me what they saw?" They stayed quiet. She rolled her eyes and said, "Fine. I'll go check myself. Which way was it?"

Ouch!—she yelped in surprise and stopped walking before she could take a third step away from the creek. Nathan grabbed her upper arm with a tight grip, digging his fingers into her soft flesh. He gazed into her eyes and she gazed into his. She saw the fear and death in his eyes. He was gone for less than thirty minutes, less than a quarter mile away from the creek, but his eyes had changed. He had the eyes of a traumatized war veteran.

Nathan said, "You *don't* want to go out there. You *don't* want to see what we've seen. Trust me, it will haunt you for the rest of your life." He leaned closer to her, so Dylan wouldn't hear him. In a soft, squeaky voice, he said, "The blood, the gore, the stench, the flies... I still hear them buzzing around my damn ears. Please don't go."

Mariah said, "Yeah, okay. I get it. But I might be able to help you if you just told me what you saw. Talking helps, guys." Yet, the men couldn't talk about it. Mariah sighed, then she said, "I'm here if you need me. Whatever happened... I guess it doesn't matter right now. We need fresh water, food, and rescue. What's the next step in our plan? Are we making more signals around here or are we going to start some fires?"

Cole said, "We're going to go back to our camp, we're going to grab our stuff, then we're going to cross this creek. We'll search for more water and food, other survivors, and... and civilization. If rescue won't come to us, we'll go to them. But we will move *that* way." He pointed at the river and asked, "Are we in agreement?"

"Yes," Michael said.

Nathan stuttered, "Y–Yeah."

Mariah and Dylan didn't have any other options. The group returned to their camp near the pond and collected their supplies. They didn't say another word about the dead bodies in the jungle.

***

"Do you think they're even searching for us?" Mariah asked as she grabbed the pea coat from her makeshift tent. "I'm guessing it's been over twenty-four hours since the crash. A day and a half, maybe. When a plane goes down, the entire world is usually rushing to help. The Americans, the French, the Germans... Where are they now?"

Cole grabbed a duffel bag and said, "It might be the weather, it could be something political. I don't know how this works. I really don't. I just know: *eventually*, someone will come looking."

"Eventually... that doesn't sound urgent at all."

"You asked, and I gave you my opinion. What else do you want from me?"

"I want you to stop acting so... so nonchalant about all of this. I get that you want to be the great 'leader,' our savior who will be all over the news when we get home, but your optimism isn't helping. Your lying isn't helping."

"Lying? *Lying?* When have I ever lied to you?"

Michael approached with his hands raised. He said, "Let's all calm down. Come on, we don't have time for this. We have to get to the other side of the creek."

Mariah nodded at Michael and said, "About that. Maybe it's not a lie, but you're withholding the truth. All of you are. And now you're pretending like everything's going to be okay. It's bullshit."

Cole responded, "We're trying to protect you and–"

"I don't need your goddamn protection! I need to know what's–"

A shriek ripped through the misty rainforest.

They glanced back and spotted Dylan being dragged into the jungle, kicking at a bush while trying to fight off his captor.

Michael yelled, "Dylan!"

He stumbled forward, falling to his knees once and then twice as he slid across the muddy ground. He jumped through the bush and gave chase. Nathan ran after them, but before he could reach the trees, darts hit the ground in front of him, striking the dirt with dull *thud* sounds. Dipped in frog poison, the darts were made of wood and thistle. He watched as two darts hit Michael's back, but the man didn't stop running. He followed the sound of his son's screaming and weeping, even as the noise dwindled.

Nathan's eyes widened as he spotted the people in the trees, crouching on the thick branches and partially obscured by the leaves. The men were thin but strong. Using dye from crushed annatto seeds and extracted jenipapo, their copper-colored skin was decorated with red and black paint in order to incite fear amongst their enemies. Most of them only wore thin loincloths to cover their groins. They belonged to an indigenous tribe—*an uncontacted group*. They used long blowguns to shoot darts at Michael.

Through the mist and the drizzle, Nathan noticed other figures on the branches. The tribesmen surrounded their campsite.

Nathan shouted, "The trees! They're in the trees!"

Cole took cover behind a tree trunk. Just as he turned the corner, a dart penetrated the top of his hand. He felt the wood *cracking* his third metacarpal bone, right at the center of his hand. He hid behind the tree, fell to his ass, and then he grabbed the dart. But he stopped himself before he could pull it out. He knew it was poisoned, but he didn't know if removing the dart would save him or kill him.

"Oh shit, oh shit," he muttered.

Mariah crawled into one of the makeshift tents. She threw the pea coat over her body and screeched. She heard the darts hitting the branches and twigs around her.

Nathan stood in front of the pond and yelled, "Wait! Please stop! Don't do this! We don't want to do this! Please!"

In the jungle, Michael leaned against a tree and breathed noisily. He didn't feel any pain from the darts in his back, he didn't notice them at all, but he was woozy and confused. His clothing was soaked in a cold sweat, his skin reddened, and his throat tightened. He lurched forward, pushing through the sudden delirium.

He mumbled, "Dylan... Dylan, dad–daddy's coming. Please... don't... don't hurt my... my son."

A gunshot echoed through the jungle. A flock of birds flew skywards, a troop of monkeys babbled and swung away on the branches, and a herd of capybaras ran through the jungle.

Michael collapsed, hitting the ground face-first. He squeezed his eyes shut, struck the ground with the bottom of his fists, and screamed in pain. He was shot in the calf with a shotgun, the lead pellets easily tearing through his pants and muscle. He looked back at his leg, then he closed his eyes and screamed again.

The sight was horrific. Blood drenched his pant leg and even flowed into his sock. Through the holes on his pants, he saw parts of his mangled calf. There were at least ten tiny holes scattered across the back of his leg. There was a larger hole towards the center of the shotgun blast. In that large hole, he saw his butchered muscle. It was bloody with slits of white, and it pulsated like a heart.

He tried to crawl forward, but he could barely move. The pain neutralized him. He searched for Dylan and his captor, but he couldn't see much through his teary, blurred vision.

He whispered, "Jennifer, I'm sorry."

Nathan ran to Cole's side. He shouted, "We have to go!"

"Go without me," Cole said as he pushed him away.

"That was a gunshot, man! Stop trying to play the damn hero! I'm not leaving you!"

"Just go without me!"

"Cole, you're coming with me. I'll carry you if I–"

Cole raised his hand up to Nathan's face, showcasing the dart in his hand. Then he pointed down at his busted ankle.

He said, "I weigh two-hundred-and-twenty pounds. My ankle is fucked and I got hit with one of their darts. I'm feeling lightheaded and... and sleepy. You can't carry me. If you try, you'll die. Run, Nathan. Get out of here before it's too late." Nathan shook his head, awed by his courage. Cole shoved him and yelled, "Survive!"

His teary eyes glowing with fear and reluctance, Nathan ran back to the campsite. He grabbed Mariah's leg and pulled her out of the tent.

Mariah yelled, "No! Please no! I don't want to die!"

"Mariah, stop it! It's me, it's Nathan! Get up! We have to go!"

Mariah tossed the pea coat aside and looked up at Nathan with wide, bulging eyes. She glanced over at Cole. Cole nodded at her, as if to say: *go on, run.* Mariah jumped up to her feet. Nathan grabbed her hand and led her into the jungle. He took one last glance back at the campsite. Between the trees, he saw Cole swinging a branch at one of the tribesmen. Then, a dart struck Cole's neck. The man passed out after swinging the branch once more.

Nathan and Mariah barreled through the jungle. They heard the darts hitting the trees around them, slicing through the leaves on the bushes, and thudding on the ground. They saw spider monkeys, capybaras, and exotic birds moving through the jungle with them. They spotted a large anaconda wrapped around a tree, too. They hoped it would attack the tribesmen and protect them, although the snake also struck fear into their hearts.

As they turned and ran past a tree, Mariah's legs were caught in a bola. She yelped as she plummeted to the floor. Her legs became entangled by the thick cords.

"Nathan!" she yelled as she rolled onto her back. "Help me! Don't leave me!"

Nathan dropped to his knees and slid to her side,

like a soccer player after scoring a goal. He examined her legs. The bola was made of thick, durable vines and weighed down with heavy stones. Due to Mariah's frantic kicking and screaming, he couldn't concentrate. He tugged on the vines, which caused him to inadvertently tighten the bola.

"You have to stop kicking," he said.

"Just get it off of me! Please!"

"I'm trying, but you–"

He stopped and glanced over his shoulder. He didn't hear darts or tree branches. He heard rapid footsteps and male voices. And the voices grew louder with each step.

He stammered, "I–I–I'm sorry. I don–don't know wha–what to do. I can't stay. I can't..." As he ran off, he yelled, "I'm sorry!"

"No! No, don't leave me! Please, Nathan! I'm scared! I'm so fucking scared! Oh my God, don't leave me!"

Nathan sprinted as fast as possible. He wanted to run away from the tribesmen as much as he wanted to run away from Mariah's pained voice. His brain throbbed so hard that he felt each pulsation against his skull. A burning sensation spread across his legs. His heart pounded against his chest, causing the pain from his broken rib to intensify. He believed his heart would burst out of his chest at any moment, as if he were a character in a cartoon. But he couldn't stop running.

Survive—he heard Cole's final word in his head.

Then Mariah stopped screaming. He was struck by an overwhelming sensation of déjà vu. It felt like the moment he awoke strapped to his seat on the branch. He felt scared, sick, and alone. He wasn't grateful to be alive. Truth be told, he would have preferred it if they had caught him first. But he kept fighting for survival—maybe it was Cole's final word, maybe it was the human's natural will to live.

Nathan juked behind a tree, then he slid down into a ditch. From head-to-toe, he covered himself in goops of mud, twigs, and stones. He left a small gap in front of his nose so he could breathe. He squinted up at the trees. He saw the final rain drops plummeting down on him as the drizzle came to its end. *No more rain,* he thought, *I'm begging you, don't let it rain again.*

He felt claustrophobic under the thick mud—hot, trapped, *cornered.* His nostrils flared with each panicked breath, amplifying the pain in his chest. The heat from his legs spread across his entire body. The sensation was so hot that he believed the mud would melt. His heartbeat was loud and powerful. Like the bass from a car's subwoofer, he thought his heartbeat could shake the floor.

He shuddered as a tribesman walked past the ditch. He held his breath and clenched his jaw. His eyes darted to the right. Another tribesman walked around the tree behind him. They moved slowly as they searched for him. They communicated with each other, but Nathan didn't understand their language or their gestures.

After thirty seconds, Nathan clenched his fist. His lungs hankered after a breath of fresh air. The tribesman slid into the ditch. He stepped on Nathan's stomach, unaware of the survivor's presence in the mud. Nathan gritted his teeth and fought the urge to gasp. His arms shook, but his movements went unnoticed.

The tribesman said something to his peer as he climbed out of the ditch. They appeared to be discussing Nathan and his disappearance, but they didn't sound frustrated. The hunters retreated, their footsteps fading away within seconds, but Nathan continued to hold his breath—ninety seconds, *two minutes.*

Then he gasped for air. He slapped his hands over his mouth to try to smother the noise of his panting and weeping. Relief didn't siphon the anxiety from his body or remove the burden from his shoulders. Instead, guilt climbed onto his shoulders and tormented him, whispering four names into his ears: *Cole, Mariah, Michael, Dylan.*

He crawled out from under the mud. He was dizzy because of the lack of oxygen, but he stayed on his feet. He teetered around and examined his surroundings. He didn't know his location and he didn't know how to survive on his own. He looked at the footsteps behind the trees to his left and right. If he avoided the footsteps, he could avoid the tribe. By doing so, he would be abandoning his fellow survivors.

He sighed, then he whispered, "No, no, no. I can't leave you behind. I have to do something. It's dangerous, but I couldn't live with myself if I walked away. I have to *try* to make it right." As he followed the footsteps, covered in mud and twigs, he said,

"Holly, Kyle, I'm sorry, but I need to do this. For them, for you, for myself. Shit, I'm so sorry."

Chapter Eight

The Tribe

Nathan trudged through the jungle, Mariah's muddy pea coat draped over his head. Nighttime arrived with another drizzle, but the Amazonian heat lingered—*eighty degrees Fahrenheit*. He kept his head low, eyes on the ground, as he attempted to follow the footprints. The rain, however, caused small mudslides, which wiped out some of their tracks. A few of the tribesmen also covered their footmarks. They were smart hunters. The nighttime darkness didn't help, either.

As he flicked the spark wheel of an old Bic lighter, he muttered, "What was I thinking? I'm going to get myself lost out here. Well, shit, I was already lost anyway, but this is just crazy. Where are they?"

He heard a *snapping* twig. He turned quickly and held the lighter over his head. The flame barely illuminated the tree and the bush to his right, then a single raindrop extinguished the fire. Yet, he still stood there with the lighter over his head. He gazed into the pitch-black darkness beyond the trees in front of him.

And he felt something—or someone—staring back at him.

He had spent nearly two days in the jungle. He knew the rainforest, a biome filled with life, had a breath of its own. It breathed through its plants, its water, and its inhabitants. But his mind wouldn't allow him to pin the blame on nature. Paranoia told him the tribesmen were stalking him through the jungle.

"I'm walking into a trap, aren't I?" he whispered. He flicked the spark wheel and ignited the lighter. Holding the fire close to his chest, he marched forward and said, "But I can't turn back. They need me. Come on, Nathan, you can do this."

He traveled through the rainforest for another ten minutes. He slipped on mud, he became tangled in vines, and he avoided the snakes, monkeys, and armadillos in the jungle. He followed the trail of footprints and the collapsed bushes. He guessed his peers were carried or dragged through the bushes as the tribesmen returned to their home.

As he slunk past a snake on a tree, a faint shout echoed towards him. He heard a second shout. It was a scream of agony, and the voice belonged to a man.

"Cole? Michael?" he said with a furrowed brow. "What are they doing to you?"

He followed the voice, treading on the heels of suffering. The jungle was wet—rain rolling down tree trunks, hanging onto plants, glistening on the mud— but he saw himself descending into hell. He crouched down as the shouting grew louder. He made his way up a steep hill.

"Michael," he said in awe as he recognized the voice.

"You bastards!" Michael shouted. "Oh God, it burns! It burns!"

Nathan trembled in fear. He heard the pain in the man's strained voice. He gasped as he reached the top of the hill. He dropped to the ground and wrapped the pea coat around his body. He found that he wasn't on top of a natural hill. He was on a large, slanted stone covered in moss and mud. He crawled up to the edge of the stone. There was a small pond in front of him.

The tribe's camp lay beyond the pond. Eight huts, made of palm leaves and wood, formed a circle around the camp. Some of their hammocks were visible through their doorless entrances. Beyond the huts, a large shack appeared to serve as a cafeteria and a community center. Around the campsite, the tribespeople planted manioc, sweet potato, corn, and other crops. They gathered fruit from the jungle, too.

The people were isolated, they didn't rely on modern technology or medicine, but they survived in the rainforest. The tribe and their camp would have surprised Nathan on any other day. Their mere existence was fascinating. That night, in the jungle, he could only focus on his fellow survivors. In particular, his eyes were glued to Michael.

He cried, "I'm sorry it took me so long. I wanted to help, but I don't know what to do. Please, man, don't die. I–I'm trying my best. I'm just… I'm scared."

***

Nude, Michael was tied to a crownless tree trunk with durable twine at regular intervals—around his ankles, his knees, his thighs, his waist, his ribs, and his chest. His wrists were tied together behind the trunk, but his hands were at least a foot away from each other. His feet didn't touch the ground. His toes hung over a lit cooking pit—*an earth oven.*

The intense heat from the earth oven turned his feet red. The skin under his toes began to peel. A few droplets of blood trickled from the peeling skin and plopped on the firewood in the pit. The blood *sizzled* for a few seconds, but the sound was drowned out by the screaming and chattering and laughing at the camp.

The large toenail on his left foot cracked, then another toenail shattered—and then another. The gummy flesh under his toenails was aggravated by the heat, too. The pain was unbearable.

Splinters from the tree trunk entered the gunshot wounds on his calf, which caused his leg to shake violently. And, when his leg shook, his calf scraped the trunk, leading to *more* pain and *more* shaking. It was a never-ending cycle of suffering. At the very least, he found some relief in the fact that he wasn't forced to stand on his own.

Cole, Mariah, and Dylan sat in a jail cell near the pond. The cell's bars were made of sturdy wood with about four inches of space between each. Mariah sat on the ground in the corner of the cell. Dylan was unconscious, his head on her lap. He fainted every time he heard his father's screaming. It was as if he were living vicariously through him, sharing his pain. Cole gripped the bars and screamed at the tribespeople. He begged them for mercy while simultaneously cursing them for the capture and torture.

A thirty-six-year-old woman sat in the other corner of the cell, her arms crossed over her exposed breasts. Her blonde hair was flecked with mud and blood, but she wasn't lacerated. She was tall, so her long legs could reach the other side of the cell if she stretched. Black bags hung under her dull blue eyes.

She hadn't slept in days.

All of the prisoners were stripped of their clothing while they were unconscious.

"Fuck, fuck, fuck," Cole said as he whimpered. He turned around, leaned back against the bars, and asked, "What the hell is going on here?"

Stroking Dylan's cheek, Mariah glared at the other woman and asked, "And who the hell are you?"

The sides of the woman's mouth rose into a smile, then fell into a frown, then one side rose to form a smirk, and then she frowned again. She didn't know how to react. She appreciated the company, but the torture was shocking. She couldn't mute Michael's screaming.

In a soft voice, like a child's, she said, "My name is… Christina Hernandez. I–I'm like… like you, I think."

"You were on the plane?" Mariah asked.

"Yes, yes," Christina said, eager yet hesitant. "I was a–a flight attendant on the plane. We–We were going to São Paulo. That plane, right? You guys are talking about that plane?"

Mariah and Cole nodded.

Christina continued, "I, um… I have no idea how I survived that, but I did. *We* did. There were… others."

Cole asked, "Where are they now? Can they help us?"

"No. No, they can't. I woke up somewhere… somewhere out there. I met a man named Clark and a woman. But, um… Well, I can't remember her name. I know it's not right, but I just can't remember. Can you believe that? If I survive, if I escape this place… I can't give her family closure. And if I die here, who'll give my family closure? You'll forget me just like I forgot her, right? My husband, my little girl, they won't know what happened to me. I'll be forgotten."

She held her hands over her ears, closed her eyes, and sobbed. The screaming drilled into her ears and cut through her brain.

She yelled, "Damn it! I'm in hell!" She lowered her hands and stared down at the ground between her grubby feet. Grimacing, she said, "Yeah, that's probably right. Maybe I'm already dead, huh? Maybe this really is hell. Or maybe it's just better this way. If they torture me like that, I don't want my baby girl to find out about it. I just want to disappear like the rest of them. I want 'em to take me into that jungle and bury me somewhere I can't be found..."

Cole and Mariah gave her a moment to mumble to herself—to collect herself. They understood her fear, doubt, and grief. They all went through it.

After a minute of quiet weeping, Cole said, "Talk to us. What happened after you met Clark and that woman? We deserve to know, Christina."

Christina nodded and sniffled, then she said, "You're right. You deserve our side of the story. It might be helpful, right? Okay, so, um... We found each other just a few minutes after we crashed. I swear, there were still burning pieces of the plane falling from the sky. And people... people raining down into the jungle from the stormy skies, like Rapture's rejects..." She took another moment to calm herself. She said, "We grouped up. Me, Clark, and... 'the woman.' We agreed that I'd build the camp while they went out to look for supplies. They did one run and then another, and everything was fine. I was feeling good about it. I thought we were going to survive. Then, everything went black while I was eating fruit by myself at our camp. I woke up in this cell."

Cole asked, "Did they ever tell you *why* they captured you? Do they speak English?"

"No. We tried to communicate with them. That woman, she tried speaking Spanish to them. Nothing. I tried speaking English and a little bit of Portuguese. *Nothing.* We came up with our own theory, though."

"What happened? Why are they doing this?"

"Clark said it was a misunderstanding."

"A misunderstanding?" Mariah repeated in disbelief. "They shot us with darts, they took our clothes and locked us up, and they're *torturing* Michael because of a misunderstanding? Really?"

Christina responded, "That was the theory. It's what Clark told me. While they were out looking for supplies, they... they found a dying boy in the woods. He looked like them, like these people. Apparently, he was hit by a piece of the wreckage. They tried to save the kid, but... but..." She paused to swallow the lump in her throat. She said, "But the little boy died in Clark's arms. Clark said some of the tribe members spotted them with the dead body. He tried to explain himself to them, but they didn't understand or I guess they just didn't want to listen. That's why they took us, that's why they're torturing us. We're being blamed and punished for that boy's death."

Mariah cried, "We had nothing to do with that! We weren't anywhere near you! This is your fault!"

"Mariah, don't," Cole said. "Now's not the time for that."

"But we didn't do anything! We're innocent..."

"I know, I know. But we won't make any progress by attacking each other now. We have to stick together. It's our only choice."

Mariah stared down at Dylan and watched as her tears dripped onto his face. Christina crawled closer to her corner and apologized repeatedly. Michael continued screaming, simultaneously combative and desperate. Dylan did not awaken during the conversation.

Cole examined the tribespeople and thought about Christina's story. He remembered the mutilated bodies they had discovered in the jungle. He nearly asked: *were their genitals mutilated? Were her eyes gouged out? Were his nipples torn off?* But he already knew the answer. They found Clark and the nameless woman in a grave in the jungle. It wasn't the type of closure Christina sought for her family.

He said, "We can't give up. Rescue is on the way. I know it. They wouldn't leave us out here."

He watched as a group of men circled the crownless tree trunk. Some of them appeared jovial, chattering and laughing. A few of them were angry, wearing scowls and snarling at Michael. Some of the younger tribesmen gathered at the shack, along with some women and children. They were disgusted by the torture.

Cole said, "I think Clark was right. We can't blame these people. We fell from the sky with a big, powerful explosion. We landed in their home, bringing fire and death and destruction with us. Like I said before, we look and sound like invaders. It's all bad luck, bad timing. We just need a damn rescue team to find us. That's all."

As she wiped her tears off Dylan's rosy cheeks, Mariah said, "Maybe it's because of them. Maybe there's some sort of 'preservation' law that's stopping them from bulldozing in here and saving us. I've read about it before, you know? We're not supposed to be here. These people don't have our immune systems, our vaccines, our modern medicine. By landing here, by sticking our noses where they didn't belong, we probably contaminated this entire area and all of its people. We... Jesus Christ, we could be the reason this tribe is wiped out. Whether we meant it or not, we're their exterminators."

As he watched Michael, a profound sense of regret and sadness in his eyes, Cole said, "And now they're exterminating us. They're making an example of us. 'If you invade us, we'll butcher you.' That's the message." The women sniveled, saddened by the truth. Cole said, "We don't stand a chance against them right now. Mariah, Christina, you two can probably make a run for it if the opportunity presents itself, but the boy and I aren't getting out of here. His leg, my ankle... We can only hope for the best."

Mariah said, "I wasn't planning on abandoning you anyway. I can't leave Dylan like this."

"Yeah, I thought so. You're a good person, Mariah. You're going to be a great teacher when you get back home. Things look hopeless, but we still have a chance of getting out of here. Don't forget, Nathan is still out there."

Mariah raised her head slowly. She ran her eyes

over every inch of the small cell. *Dylan, Cole, Christina*—she counted her cellmates, as if she were taking roll for a class. A tender smile stretched across her face. Truth be told, she forgot about Nathan after she awoke at the camp, nude and sweaty. He was the last person on her mind, but now he was the most important person in her life.

"He can save us," she whispered, a spark of hope glinting in her eyes.

Christina asked, "Who's Nathan?"

Cole responded, "He's another survivor. He was with us when they attacked, but I don't know what happened to him. The last time I saw him, he was running away."

"And the last time *I* saw him, he ditched me," Mariah said. "But I don't blame him. It was a hopeless situation, so he did the right thing. As long as he comes back for us, I'll forgive him."

His eyes on Michael, Cole said, "I have a feeling he got away safely. I don't think he'll abandon us, either. He's good people. And, as of right now, he's our best bet for survival."

Chapter Nine

Odontomachus

"Let me go!" Michael shouted. "Please don't do this! You're killing me! It hurts! Why?! Why are you doing this? Please! Someone help!"

The tips of Michael's toes turned black. The skin around the burn marks was a bright red, the color fading towards his heels. The blood stopped dripping from his peeling skin, as if his feet were completely drained. The pain from his toes began to subside. Instead, the pain moved across his soles towards his heels and up into his ankles.

A strong, bald tribesman, his face decorated with red and black paint, approached Michael. He held a large branch in his hand, like a golf club. He tapped Michael's right ankle. Michael gritted his teeth as a jolt of pain surged into his mutilated calf and his burned foot. Blood squirted out of one of the gunshot wounds.

The tribesman pointed the branch at Michael's injured leg. He said something, but Michael couldn't catch it due to the language barrier and the pain reverberating through his body. But he understood the gesture. The man referenced his leg for some reason, speaking as if he were planning something. Then, one of the younger tribesmen grabbed a branch from the ground and ran off into the jungle.

Michael stuttered, "Wha–What are you going to–"

The tribesman struck his leg at the shin five times.

He didn't use enough force to snap the bone, that wasn't his goal, but each strike pushed Michael's pellet-riddled calf against the gnarled ridges of the tree trunk. Michael convulsed, but he could barely move. He felt a tingly sensation in his leg, as if a hundred ants were marching *into* his flesh.

Bug-eyed, Cole was awed by the torture. He had never seen anything like it before—and he knew it was barely beginning.

He said, "Mariah, turn around and cover the boy's face. If he wakes up, don't you let him look this way. Whatever you do, do *not* let him look at this."

"What are they doing to him? Why are they hitting him like that?"

"Just trust me. I don't hear any planes, helicopters, or rescue teams. So, this is going to get worse before it gets better and there's nothing we can do about it now. But you can block it out. Turn around. Protect him and yourself, Mariah."

As Michael screamed again, Christina turned around and faced the pond. She gripped the wooden bars, her empty gaze fixed on the water.

She said, "Trust him. I've seen it before and it's... it's the worst thing I've ever experienced in my life. It's not like the movies, it's not like the tragedies people post on Twitter. It's real. Even if they change their methods, it will still be horrifying. So fuckin' horrifying. I haven't slept since the crash, but it's not because we landed here. It's because I still see their faces when I close my eyes. I'd cover my ears, but their screaming is still echoing in my head. Once you *see* and *hear* something like that, it never goes away. Never, never, never..."

Mariah lifted Dylan's head from her legs, she turned around, then she returned his head to her lap. She caressed his face and rocked back-and-forth.

Cole kept his eyes on Michael. He needed to keep his eyes open at all times in order to stay informed. He couldn't save himself and the group with his eyes closed. He noticed the strong tribesman wasn't trying to hurt Michael with the branch. Each hit was painful, but there was more to it. The way he pointed at Michael, the way he spoke to the other tribesmen... He was a leader, and he was directing.

"Oh my God," Cole whispered as he spotted the young tribesman returning from the jungle.

The end of the young man's branch was coated in honey. Dozens of carnivorous trap-jaw ants— *odontomachus*—skittered around the wood and consumed the honey. Black and dark brown, the ants averaged about a centimeter in length. Their jaws *snapped* at the wood, bites strong enough to crack the branch.

The leader pointed at Michael's leg, he nodded, and he said something—*do it.* The young tribesman struck Michael's ankles with the honey-coated end of the branch, cycling between left and right.

The trap-jaw ants crawled up Michael's legs. Most of them landed on his right leg, though. The ants moved with unbelievable speed. Some of the ants zoomed up from his ankles to his thighs in the blink of an eye. The heat from the earth oven scared them into speeding up his body. Many of the ants were attracted to his blood.

The ants marched over to the gunshot wound on

his calf. They snapped their jaws at his exposed muscle, tearing through the fibrous tissue with ease. The other ants bit into his legs and created fresh wounds across his shins, thighs, and waist. Blood streamed out of the small bite marks, rolling down his body like raindrops on a window.

Michael's eyes widened and retreated into his skull as he watched the fierce ants. He had never seen ants like those before. He squirmed and flinched with each bite. He clenched his jaw until his teeth cracked, jolts of pain shooting into the roots of his teeth and reverberating across his gums.

He could only wheeze and cry. He didn't want to scream because he didn't want to awaken his son or disturb his fellow survivors. But the pain from his calf and teeth was too much to endure. After thirty seconds, he felt a chunk of his calf muscle fall out of his leg—*dangling.*

He unleashed a bloodcurdling shriek. He convulsed against the tree trunk as the ants entered the pellet wounds and devoured his muscle.

"Pl–Please, please, pl–pl–please," he croaked out. "Why? Why? Wh–Why? Why are you–"

His eyes rolled back, his head spun, then he fainted. His head dangled down, his chin against his chest. The leader slapped his cheeks gently while the young tribesman tapped his shins with the branch. They wanted to wake him up. After all, torture wasn't very effective when the victim was unconscious.

Cole barked, "Stop! Stop it! You're killing him! Oh, Jesus Christ, how can you do this to another human being? We're people like you, goddammit! Can't you see that? Let him go!"

The tribe ignored him. A young man approached the pond with a bucket. He filled the bucket with water, then he returned to the crownless tree. Taking turns, the men used cups to splash water on Michael's face.

Dylan's eyes fluttered open, the crust crumbling off his eyelashes. He saw Mariah sobbing over him, eyes closed with one hand over her mouth. He heard Christina's weeping from the other corner of the cell. He felt the vibrations of the cell bars as Cole struck and shook the wood in anger. He didn't hear his father, though.

He knew they were torturing him, he was unconscious because he couldn't listen to his father's agony, but he didn't hear his voice anymore. His silence was worrying. Silence meant absence, silence meant death. Slowly, he lifted his head from Mariah's lap and sat up. Mariah didn't notice until it was too late. She tried to grab him, but he slipped out of her fingers.

Dylan crawled up to the cell bars beside Cole and yelled, "Daddy!"

He spotted the monstrous ants gnawing on his flesh from afar. He saw the vertical lines of blood flowing down his body, almost parallel. And he noticed his father wasn't responding. *Dead*—the worst possibility immediately crept into his mind. *My dad is dead,* he thought. He released the bars and fell back, unconscious.

Mariah caught him before he could hit the ground. She apologized to his unconscious body as she dragged him back to the corner of the cell. She caught a glimpse of Michael's torture, but she didn't see everything. She saw black blots moving around his body. She didn't know they were ants. She thought they were leeches. Either way, it was an awful way to die.

Without taking his eyes off Michael, Cole said, "Don't let him see this again. It's not over yet..."

Michael awoke with a gasp, the water dripping from his face like Gatorade off an athlete's face in a commercial. He breathed deeply through his nose and glared at the leader. His eyes drifted towards the jail cell. He saw his fellow survivors in all their nude glory, sobbing and panicking, but he could only see his son's limp legs. Just like Dylan, the worst possibility entered his mind: *my son is dead.*

Through his clenched teeth, flinching with each ant bite, he said, "You sick bastards. If you hurt my son... I'll kill all of your children. You savages, you animals... I'm going to kill you."

The leader stared at him with a steady expression. He couldn't be shaken or stirred by the threats. He had the upper hand—and he didn't understand a single word out of Michael's mouth. He snapped his fingers at the other tribesmen.

"Wha–What are you doing? Huh? What else can you do to me? I'm being eaten alive by fucking ants, you cunt! You can't–"

A tribesman thrust a spear into Michael's ribcage from the side. The flint spearhead slipped past the center of his ribcage and scraped his lung. The spearhead slid out with a *squelching* sound, followed by a geyser of blood. Another tribesman thrust a spear into Michael's abdomen. The spearhead cut into his intestines. He twirled the staff while the spearhead was still inside of him, as if he were drilling into him. His sliced and mutilated intestines became entangled—there was a *real* knot in his stomach.

The tribesmen took turns stabbing him with the spears. One of them thrust the spear upward near his neck. The spearhead tore through his chest and broke through his collarbone. The other spear entered his stomach at the belly button. Once again, the tribesman twirled the staff and twisted his insides. The spearhead *plopped* out of his stomach along with a piece of his intestines. The organ hung out of him, swinging down by his pubic hair.

The tribesmen stabbed his biceps, his thighs, his chest, and his sides. Blood squirted out of the wounds as he twitched and screamed. A tribesman thrust the spear into his ribcage again. The flint spearhead shattered a rib and ruptured a lung, ending the shouting in a second. He pushed and pulled on the shaft, fucking him with the spear.

Michael coughed up a drizzle of blood. Foamy blood and saliva bubbled out of his mouth, frothing like a cappuccino.

The leader lit a branch on fire. He used the heat from the torch to lead the trap-jaw ants towards Michael's gaping wounds. Some of the ants entered his abdomen, others marched into his chest through his ribcage. A few of the ants escaped onto the tree trunk and flung themselves away. A group of kids nearby yelled and giggled, as if they were high school students at a haunted house attraction—*fun, fun, fun.*

Michael couldn't handle the pain. Struggling to breathe, he fell unconscious again. The twine kept him close to the tree trunk, his back riddled with scrapes.

The leader slapped him, threw a cup of water at his face, and said something to him. Although he spoke a different language, the message was clear: *wake up.* But Michael stayed unconscious. A string of bloody drool hung from his lip. He snorted and hiccupped, like a drunk knocked out during a street brawl. Blood began to ooze out of his nostrils.

Cole watched as the tribesmen discussed the situation. The leader reached into a basket and retrieved a knife—sharpened flint tied to a short stick.

Barely audible, he said, "Just finish it already."

The leader slapped Michael again, but it was ineffective. He laughed as he slapped his loose scrotum, watching as the testicles swung from side-to-side like Newton's cradle. He kept laughing as he stabbed the side of Michael's scrotum. He glided the blade downward at an angle, then inward towards the center of his scrotum, creating a large, curved gash.

Blood rained down onto the earth oven, sizzling on the firewood and even extinguishing some of the flames. Two trap-jaw ants entered his scrotum through the gash. They attacked his bare, vulnerable testicle. Michael awoke to the most unbearable pain. He shook his head frantically and screamed—*ahh, ahh, ahhhh!*

Cole gasped and lowered his head. His clammy palms slid down the wooden cell bars. Tears sprinkled out of his eyes with each blink. Vomit climbed into his throat, ready to explode out of his mouth. Every hair across his body prickled. He felt pins and needles *everywhere.* His head swayed a bit as he nearly fainted, but he clung to consciousness. He heard Michael's screaming, but he refused to look back.

Not yet, he told himself. *Don't do it, Cole. You can't save him anyway, so there's no point in watching him die. Just give it a few minutes. It will be over soon, then you can re-assess the situation.*

Seven minutes and thirty-four seconds.

It took exactly seven minutes and thirty-four seconds before Michael finally stopped screaming.

Cole raised his head slowly—anxious, *afraid.* He drew a short breath and shuddered. As expected, Michael died from the torture. A person could only withstand so much pain and shock.

One of his testicles burned in the earth oven, the other hung out of his open scrotum. His penis wasn't spared. Someone had slathered it in honey, attracting at least half-a-dozen trap-jaw ants. His dick was bitten so much that it was barely attached to his body, hanging from a measly piece of flesh. Blood kept pouring out of his mouth as well as the holes on his chest. His ruptured lung guaranteed a long, painful death.

As the tribesmen cut Michael down, the trap-jaw ants fell to the ground. Cole fell back as the ants ran towards them, prompting Mariah and Christina to glance over. They screamed and scrambled around the cell as some of the large ants ran past them. The rest of the ants ran around them and entered the jungle. They didn't attack the survivors.

Cole held his hand over his chest and muttered, "Jesus Christ..."

Some of the tribe members pointed and laughed at them. A few of the women appeared to be displeased, sneering and whispering amongst themselves.

Nathan lay on the stone, shocked by the violence. Unlike Cole, he saw all of the torture. He witnessed the exact moment Michael passed away. The violence terrified him and scarred his mind, so he didn't think about vengeance. He knew he had to do something to rescue the other survivors, though.

Before he could slide down, a group of kids from the tribe walked up to the edge of the stone. They crouched down beside Nathan, ate berries, threw pebbles at the pond, and chatted. They had witnessed violence before, but they never enjoyed it. The screaming discomfited them while the blood made them squeamish. They wanted to get away from it, they wanted to play, they wanted to be kids.

Nathan lay motionless. The kids didn't notice him and he could easily overpower them, but the fear flowing through his body paralyzed him. One false move and he'd die—he truly believed that.

Chapter Ten

Till Dawn

Michael's dead body was removed from the tree trunk and carried into the community center. Some of the tribespeople splashed water on the trunk and scrubbed the blood away. The light from the earth oven reached the cell, casting parallel shadows from the wooden bars. Some thick, black clouds obscured the stars, but, to the survivors' dismay, rain didn't bless the campsite.

Excessive rain often canceled school, work, and public transportation. They shared the same idea: *maybe rain can cancel a session of torture?*

With a toneless voice, Mariah asked, "What are we going to do?"

Cole looked at her, eyes glazed with tears. The jail cell had been silent since Michael's tragic death. The extreme violence temporarily wiped their vocabularies and addled their minds. They kept hearing Michael's screaming—*his begging*—in their heads. They could hear their own shrieks, too. They knew they were next, but they didn't know when or how they'd die. The mystery was frightening.

"I guess the better question is: what *can* we do?" Cole responded. "I'm not usually a downer, but we don't have a lot of options, guys. No matter how I look at it, we can't get out of here together. You and Christina can sneak out, but Dylan and I *can't* move. We'd just be a burden. We can try to break out and fight back, but we're outnumbered and we don't have any weapons. It would be suicide."

"Waiting," Mariah said. "Is that really the best we can do? We can wait until our... our deaths?"

"I hope it doesn't come to that for any of us."

As she stared at the crownless tree trunk, Christina said, "There's one way to prolong our survival. They offered me a chance to–"

Mid-sentence, the cell's gate swung open. The presumed leader pointed at Cole, then he curled his finger towards him. The gesture said: *you, come here.*

Cole glared at the man, trembling as he fought the urge to weep and beg. He thought about fighting the tribespeople, but he knew he couldn't win. He didn't want to haunt his fellow survivors by causing a scene directly in front of them. And he didn't want to traumatize Dylan by awakening him from his slumber. He nodded at the leader and accepted his fate.

Frowning, Mariah leaned forward and shouted, "Wait! We need you, Cole. Don't–"

"It's okay," Cole interrupted as he struggled to his feet. His head hit the top of the cell. He put a slick, confident smile on his face and said, "Just take care of each other. I can handle this."

"Please don't leave us."

Cole staggered out of the cell. Two tribesmen grabbed his arms and dragged him towards the center of the camp. They pushed him, causing him to fall to his knees near the earth oven. He grimaced as he spotted the crispy black testicle in the fire pit. *They picked me because I'm a man,* he thought, *they're smart, they don't want us to fight back and overpower them.*

He groaned as he stood up, his injured ankle wobbling under him. He glanced over at the cell and smiled, as if to say: *everything's going to be okay.* He covered his genitals with his hands for two reasons: he didn't want the other survivors to see his privates, and he wanted to dissuade the tribespeople from mutilating his crotch.

Five tribesmen surrounded him from every angle, unarmed but menacing.

He asked, "Do any of you speak English? Hmm? Can we talk about this?" The men did not respond. Cole said, "I don't, um... Okay, I'll just be honest with you. I don't want to die here. Michael, I didn't know him well, but I think he was a good man. *We* are good people. Okay? We're not here to hurt you or take your land or anything like that. The boy's death... It was an accident. *Ac-ci-dent.* Do you understand?"

The men remained silent.

Cole sniffled as he looked around, searching for a way out. He blinked rapidly and nodded as an idea popped into his head. He raised his right hand up to his face and pressed his fingers against his lips, then he moved his hand into his left palm with both hands facing upwards. In American sign language, it meant: *good.* He hoped it would translate well into the tribe's language.

He repeated the gesture, his hands shaking uncontrollably. Some tears rolled down his cheeks and dripped onto his palms.

"Please," he said with a soft, cracking voice. "I'm a good guy. This was a misunderstanding. Good, you see? I'm good."

Nathan heard bits and pieces of the conversation from the stone. His heart told him to fight, his brain told him to survive. He thought about grabbing one of the kids and using her as a hostage to negotiate with the tribe. But he couldn't muster the courage to move an inch. Fear controlled him. A fresh stream of urine soaked his pants and streamed down the stone. He cried without making a sound.

A tribesman ran forward and swung a branch at Cole's injured ankle. His ankle emitted a moist *crunching* sound as his bones shattered, ligaments tore, and tendon snapped. He plummeted to the ground, screaming at the top of his lungs. He curled into the fetal position and grabbed his broken ankle. The tribesman didn't care. He struck Cole's hand with all of his might.

Cole felt his index and middle fingers snapping, and he heard all of the bones in his hand cracking and popping. He kicked at the tribesman, missing him by a foot. He kicked at another tribesman, trying to keep them at bay, as if he were surrounded by a pack of rabid dogs.

"Get away from me!" he barked. "Stay the hell away from me!"

A young man ran up to him from behind, a heavy stone in his right hand. He struck the back of Cole's head with the stone—once, *twice.* The rough, jagged edge of the rock tore his head open, from his hairline to the center of his scalp. The blood painted streaks of red across his graying hair. Some of the blood dripped across his face. He was dazed by the attack.

The tribesmen carried him to a tree stump in front

of one of the huts. His upper body was sprawled against the surface of the trunk. A tribesman chuckled as he sat on his back, amused by the torture. Two men grabbed his arms and stretched them away from his body. He was restrained without any twine—just violence and men.

His eyes flickered open, droplets of blood hanging from his eyelashes. He groaned and he coughed. He now understood the true definition of a 'splitting headache.'

A young woman approached them. She couldn't have been older than twenty-one. Her skin was a reddish-brown, but she wasn't painted like the men. Her long, wavy black hair covered her perky breasts. She carried a bowl in her hands. She bowed in front of the group, then she crouched beside the tree stump.

Dazed, Cole mumbled, "Wha–What are you... What are you going to do to me?" The woman stayed silent and avoided eye contact. He asked, "Do you understand me? Can you... Can you spare me? Please, young lady, don't do anything you'll regret. I'm innocent."

The woman uncurled Cole's index finger. She grabbed a fish scale from the bowl. She pricked his fingertip directly underneath his fingernail, then she slid the fish scale across his finger, slicing him lengthwise down to his palm in one swift move. The sound of his shredding skin echoed through the camp.

Cole screamed and shook, but he couldn't slip past the men. They tightened their grips on his arms and stopped him from squirming away. Another man joined the group and pinned Cole's legs to the ground.

The woman grabbed his middle finger before he could clench his fist. She stabbed his fingertip, then she cut him down to his knuckle. She scraped his bone and severed a tendon.

The fingertips, along with the forehead, had the greatest pain acuity. The jolts of pain—following the fast rhythm of his heartbeat—shot up his arm, entered his torso, and stopped at his spinal cord. A tingling sensation ran across his spine with each twinge from his fingers. Cold sweat blended with the warm blood on his brow.

Cole panted as the woman sliced his ring and pinky fingers—*lengthwise,* from his fingertips to his palm. The immense pain vacuumed his lungs and attacked his mind. He didn't know how to process it. He had never felt so much pain. It was surreal—*otherworldly.* Begging didn't help Michael, but, lost in desperation, it was his only idea. He had to talk his way out of torture.

With a raspy voice, he stuttered, "Pl–Please, don–don't do this. I–I'm a good person. I won't hurt you. I–I would never do such a thing. Please, please, I'm begging you." He looked at his bloody, trembling hand. He smiled nervously at the young woman and said, "I can't hurt you. I'm weak, I'm pathetic. This… This isn't right. I don't want to die. Don't kill me. Please, ma'am, please."

The young woman didn't understand his words, but she comprehended his message. The fish scale fell out of her bloody fingers. She covered her mouth and cried. She said something in a different language as she ran off. The leader yelled something at her, frustrated by her lack of resolve and endurance.

Cole didn't have the opportunity to recover. The leader grabbed another fish scale from the bowl. He grabbed Cole's unharmed hand, driving his fingers into his palm, then he sawed into his fingers at the knuckles. One-by-one, his fingers fell to the ground, *thudding* on the mud. The white of his knuckles was visible, surrounded by dark red flesh. Only his thumb was spared.

The leader threw the severed fingers into the earth oven, laughing every step of the way. The young tribesmen released their grips on him, allowing Cole to move freely. They walked over to the fire pit and joined the chorus of laughter. Each syllable was clear: *ha-ha-ha.* They enjoyed the torture

Cole fell to his side, hissing and groaning and sobbing. He tried to stand up, but his ankle gave out. He hit the ground again. He stood on his knees and lifted his hands up to his face. On his left hand, deep lacerations stretched from his fingertips to his knuckles. His pinky, ring, middle, and index fingers were cut off from his right hand.

Both of his hands were covered in blood. The blood ran down his forearms and reached the crooks of his elbows. He couldn't feel it, though. His arms were numb.

A tribesman swung a branch at Cole's back. Cole grunted and fell forward. The tribesman swung it at him again, hitting his shoulder, the small of his back, and his ass. One of the men grabbed a knife from the ground, another grabbed a machete. The machete wasn't built by the tribe, though. It was stolen from a deforester.

From the cell, Mariah yelled, "Run, Cole! Leave us!"

Cole slid across the mud on his elbows and knees. He couldn't find a decent grip because of the moist ground and the blood on his forearms. A man thrust the flint blade into his sole. Cole tried to crawl forward, the handle of the knife protruding from his foot. The other man chopped at Cole's shoulder with the machete. The dull *thud* of each chop was louder than Cole's weeping.

But the attack couldn't stop him. He dragged himself towards the jail cell. *Where am I going? The pond? Can they swim? Are they afraid of water? What the hell am I thinking?*—he thought. His flight-or-fight response told him to get the hell out of there, so he moved as quickly as possible. He was slower than the trap-jaw ants, though.

A tribesman grabbed the handle of the knife and dragged him back until the blade slid out of his foot. He sat on the back of Cole's thighs and lifted his foot up to his chest. He examined his swollen ankle, his eyes narrowed and his mouth like an 'O' in curiosity. Then, he sawed into his heel cord with the knife. The flint severed his Achilles tendon. The cord snapped back into his calf while blood shot out of the cut.

Cole shrieked and slapped the ground with his palms. He twisted and turned, but he couldn't knock the tribesman off his balance.

The young man grabbed Cole's other leg. It was like grabbing a large fish out of water—wet and flopping in every direction. But, once he grabbed a hold of his foot, he sliced into his other ankle with the knife. He saw the heel cord retreat into his calf, as if there were a snake under his skin. But he wasn't finished.

While Cole convulsed and screamed, the tribesman grabbed his foot at the toes and heel. Then he twisted his foot, turning it left and right. With each turn, the cut on his ankle widened. Blood splattered on the man's chest, neck, and face. The blood, the crushed tendons, and the broken bones emitted a *crunching* sound.

The tribesman stood up. He giggled as he watched Cole's mutilated ankles. His feet swung from side-to-side, barely connected to his legs.

Cole struggled to breathe due to the pain, so he stopped screaming. He couldn't crawl forward because of his injured hands and he couldn't stand up because of his ruptured heel cords. He was completely immobilized. He writhed on the ground, trying his best to draw a satisfying breath. And there was only one thought in his mind: *this is how I die.*

Mariah finally turned around and faced the pond. She held Dylan's face close to her stomach and repeated the same sentence over and over: *don't wake up, don't wake up, don't wake up.* Christina stared at the ground. Although Cole had stopped screaming, she still heard his shouts in her head. She heard Clark, Michael, and the forgotten woman, too. It was as if her brain were recording all of their voices—all of their deaths.

The leader grabbed a handful of Cole's bloody hair and lifted his head from the mud. He raised the knife over his head and made an announcement. They didn't understand his language, but he sounded threatening. He wanted to strike fear into the hearts of his enemies. The torture and the murder were motivated by fear, punishment, and power.

The leader cut into Cole's forehead at his hairline while tugging on his hair. He pulled his scalp back until the hair at the top of his head caressed the nape of his neck. A waterfall of blood covered his entire face. Chunks of dark red flesh and pieces of his skull were visible. A handful of mud was placed on his head, covering the exposed bone and flesh, and then his scalp was pulled back over the wound.

His face hit the ground again. The soft mud bubbled around his mouth as he struggled to breathe. Blood and mud oozed out of his scalp in goops. His legs trembled involuntarily. The pain from his butchered ankles caused him to shake, and the shaking amplified the pain in his ankles, which led to more shaking. The cycle never ended.

The men tied a noose around Cole's neck. They grabbed the end of the rope and ran in circles around the crownless tree trunk. He was dragged past the jail cell, the community center, some of the huts, and then past the jail cell again—over and over *and over*. And they laughed about it, like children running and flying a kite at a park.

Cole felt the rope tightening around his neck, suffocating him slowly, but he couldn't do anything about it. He reached for his neck with both hands, as if he had forgotten that forty-percent of his fingers were missing. He dug his index and middle fingers under the rope. The wounds widened, flesh tearing like paper.

Some of the other tribespeople cheered while others retreated to their huts. The torture was controversial amongst the clan.

Cole's face turned blue, his lips became discolored, and his eyes reddened. He looked like a corpse with tears of blood. Before he could pass out, the men stopped running. They loosened the noose and allowed Cole to breathe. After a minute, they tightened the noose and ran a few laps around the camp again. They repeated the cycle: *choke, breathe, choke, breathe, choke.*

Nathan was heartbroken by the torture. Even before the crash, Cole offered his friendship and his assistance. He was a genuine, helpful, and respectful man. His prolonged torture was unbearable. The tribespeople continued to drag him through the mud until dawn. The children on the stone couldn't stay awake any longer. They went back to their huts to sleep.

Nathan breathed a sigh of relief, but he wasn't ready to make his move. *Michael, Cole, Mariah, Dylan*, he thought, *I'm sorry, I just don't know how to stop this.* He looked to his left, then to his right, then he examined the camp. He searched for a weapon. The shotgun blast rang through his head. If he could get his hands on the shotgun, he could save them all.

"Come on, where is it?" he muttered

Cole was thrown over the tree stump, his back against the wood. He mumbled incoherently, gasping for air and twitching erratically. A group of tribesmen surrounded him, a ray of early morning sunshine penetrating the trees and beaming down on them. Blankets of mist covered the jungle, swirling between the trees and bushes.

The leader stabbed the center of Cole's chest. He dragged the blade down to his epigastric region—the center of his upper abdomen. He forced his hand into the wound. He grabbed Cole's sternum with a tight grip, put his foot on the stump, then he yanked his arm back, as if he were trying to start a lawn mower. The sternum *snapped* out of his chest.

Cole's beating heart was exposed to the world. The heartbeat slowed to a stop—*thump*, one second, *thump*, two seconds, *thump*, three seconds, *thump*, and *stop.* His head rolled to the side, a motionless heart sitting in his chest. The leader widened the wound and broke some of his ribs. He cut the heart out with the knife. He stared at the heart, his eyes shining with wonder. He bounced it in his hand, like a baseball.

Smirking, he made his way to the prisoners. He extended his arm into the cell, the bloody heart in his steady hand. It wasn't his first time playing with hearts.

Mariah refused to look at Cole's heart. The gore made her stomach churn. She was as pale as Cole's corpse. For the first time in her life, she faced her own mortality. She learned about the frailty of life. If a plane crash didn't kill her, something else would. She couldn't escape death, but she could resist her captors for as long as possible.

Her eyes widened as Christina shuffled forward on her knees. Christina opened her mouth wide, then she chomped into the heart. Like raw chicken, the heart was difficult to bite through. She sank her teeth into the muscular organ and she shook her head until she tore a small piece of it off. She scooted back to her corner while chewing on the organ, blood dribbling down her chin—*Cole's blood.* She tossed her head back and swallowed it. And, with the *gulp,* fresh tears rolled down her pink cheeks.

The leader pointed at her, laughed, and called out to the tribespeople. He said something along the lines of: *she actually did it!*

"Oh my God," Mariah said, trembling with fear. "You–You ate... You actually... Oh my God."

Without looking at her, Christina said, "It's the only way to survive. I've been through this before. After they killed that woman, they offered Clark and I a piece of her... intestines, I think. I ate it because I didn't know what else to do. Clark refused. So, they took him out and they killed him, but they left me alone. So far, it's worked out in my favor. It'll help you, too. Eat it and you'll buy yourself a few hours. It might be enough time for–"

The leader struck the jail cell's bars and yelled at her—*be quiet!* He scowled and wagged the heart at Mariah—*eat it!*

Mariah said, "Keep that thing away from me, you monster. I *won't* eat it. Do you understand me? I will *not* eat it! No! Never!" She hugged Dylan, who was still unconscious, and she said, "And neither will he. Leave us alone."

The leader snarled at her and nodded, then he walked away. He joined the others at the crownless tree trunk. The men consumed the heart and had a conversation. Some of them went to their huts and slept.

Christina said, "You made a big mistake. He's dead. You should have just–"

"I should have what?" Mariah interrupted. "I should have eaten his... his heart? A man's heart? An *innocent* man's heart?"

"Innocence... That doesn't matter out here. Survival matters. That's it."

"We don't have to eat each other to survive. We can fight back. We can kill these motherfuckers before they kill us."

Christina said, "I don't know about that. We have a boy to take care of. I have a family waiting for me back home. I'll do anything to survive, even if it only buys me a few more seconds. I'd rather eat the dead than die like them. If we try to fight back, we'll just make them angry and we'll speed up our deaths. What can we do? Huh? *Nothing.* We can't do a damn thing about it. Next time they come over here, beg them for another chance and eat their offering. Please, don't leave me alone here."

Mariah felt another knot in her stomach. It wasn't disgust or fear. It was regret. She looked at the tribespeople and wished she took a bite of Cole's heart. She had morals, but she wasn't ready to die.

"What have I done?" she whispered.

Chapter Eleven

Hope

The Amazon rainforest was rich with resources, but hope wasn't one of them. The jungle, bathed in warm sunshine, was painted with lush greens and dark browns, but the atmosphere was grim. Tragedy touched every inch of the area—flatland created by rampant deforestation, wreckage and corpses littered by the crash, mutilated bodies dumped by the tribes.

But it only took a spark to ignite a beacon of hope.

Nathan stared up at the sky, his eyes wide and his mouth ajar. A black drone flew towards them. The sound of the buzzing propellers, like an amplified wasp nest, could be heard over the groaning branches. It stopped and hovered over the sea of trees. It appeared to be scanning the area. It didn't belong to a tribe or a lost traveler. It was a search-and-rescue drone.

Nathan slid down the stone until he couldn't see the camp—and the tribespeople couldn't see him. He rolled onto his back and extended his arms away from his body. He moved his arms up-and-down and his legs left-and-right, as if he were trying to make a snow angel on moss—*a moss angel.* He opened his mouth, but then he bit the tip of his tongue. He almost shouted.

He needed to capture the drone's attention, but he couldn't risk revealing himself to the tribe. *Who knows how far off the search team is? They might not be able to rescue us in time if I yell, right?*—he thought. He swung his limbs faster than before, so fast he believed he'd inadvertently light the moss on fire. He even mouthed some words at the drone: *I'm here, save us, please!*

His slow, controlled breathing escalated into full-on hyperventilation. The pain from his broken ribs re-emerged, setting his chest ablaze. His hair, like his clothing, was wet with rain and sweat.

He whispered, "Come on, come on. I'm right here, man. You can see me, can't you?"

Salvation was within his grasps. A rescue team wandered the jungle in search of survivors and evidence. Yet, he couldn't help but feel depressed and sick. He wasn't physically harmed by the tribe, but he witnessed real torture and murder. Two survivors died before his very eyes, and he felt partially responsible for their deaths. *If I had caused a diversion, if I had fought them off, if I had searched for the rescue team,* he thought, *then maybe I could have saved them.*

"I fucked up," he muttered. "At least let me feel like I saved the rest of them. We're right here, right under your noses..."

His eyes widened as the drone flew over the camp. It vanished behind some tall trees. After a few seconds, he could no longer hear its propellers.

He rolled back onto his stomach and said, "Shit, shit, shit."

He crawled up to the edge of the stone and watched the camp. Some of the tribespeople pointed up at the sky, shock stretching their faces out like modeling clay. A few kids hopped and waved at the drone, captivated by the foreign technology. The leader and a group of men gathered near the jungle at the outskirts of their camp. The surprise visit left them with cold, serious expressions on their faces.

The tribe had lived for generations in the rainforest with their primitive technology. The drone did not belong in their world. It was fascinating, especially to the younger tribespeople, but it was also threatening. The last flying object in the area exploded above them, lighting the clouds on fire while the debris killed a child from their tribe. If they didn't build it, they didn't trust it.

The leader pointed at the strong, young men—*you, you, and you.* He said something as he pointed into the jungle. The men nodded at him, then they ran into a shack. After a few seconds, they emerged with weapons. Two men carried bows and arrows, one man carried a hatchet and a spear. They ran into the jungle and chased after the drone.

Nathan watched the men until they disappeared behind some trees and bushes. He glanced over at the crownless tree trunk. The other tribesmen gathered around the tree while occasionally looking over at the jail cell. Nathan had seen enough to recognize their gestures. The drone wasn't going to stop the men from punishing their prisoners.

Fists clenched in frustration, he stared at the jail cell and whispered, "I have to do something. I can't sit here and wait for them to kill you. I can't wait for them to find me and kill me, too. I can't fight them all, so... so..." His eyes widened as he formulated his own idea. He said, "I have to meet them halfway. Yeah, I have to find the rescue team and bring them here. I can still save you."

He slid down the stone. He rose to his feet at the bottom of the slanted rock, his legs shaking under him. He crouched his way around the camp, creeping past the bushes and trees. He found three sets of footprints behind a shack. He took one final glance at the camp. He heard Mariah's crying. *No, not crying,* he thought, *begging, she's begging.*

He questioned his decision. He planned on finding the rescue team and leading them back to the camp, but he felt like he was abandoning the other survivors and running away from his problems.

"Fuck," he said. "I'm sorry, but I'll be back. Distract them, fight back, just buy as much time as possible. It's almost over."

He shook his head and followed the trail of footprints.

Chapter Twelve

Don't Look, Don't Listen

"Get your hands off of me!" Mariah yelled, squirming and kicking. "Don't fucking touch me! Let go! Let me go!"

"No!" Dylan cried. "Don't hurt her!"

He grabbed Mariah's arm and tried to pull her back. A tribesman kicked him in the chest, launching him back to the corner of the cell. Two tribesmen lifted Mariah from the ground, struggling to control her flailing limbs. Dylan ran forward again. His fingers slid off Mariah's muddy forearm. Christina grabbed him and pulled him back into the cell. The cell's hatch fell closed, and a sturdy branch was used to lock it.

"Why? Why won't you let me help?" Dylan cried out. "She's my friend. She's like… like my mommy. I don't want them to hurt her. Not like daddy. Please help her."

Tears in her eyes, Christina said, "I'm sorry, honey. We can't do anything right now. If we fight, they'll hurt us. Mariah, she's your friend, right?" Dylan nodded. Christina smiled and said, "Good, good. She wouldn't want you to get hurt for her. She cares about you, just like your mommy. Just… Just don't watch."

"But she's in trouble!"

"I know, I know. But you shouldn't watch this. You're young, honey. God, you're so young. You shouldn't have to go through something like this.

Why? Why are we here?"

Dylan gazed into Christina's eyes, baffled. He was nine years old, he didn't have an answer to her question. But he listened to her and he accepted her request. He placed his cheek against her breast and looked over at the center of the camp, sad and scared. Christina stared at the floor and kept repeating the same word: *why, why, why.* She entered a seemingly inescapable state of fear and denial.

Mariah was pushed up against the crownless tree trunk, men holding her arms, legs, breasts, and hips, like a gang of gropers and rapists on a crowded train in a porno.

The leader stepped forward. He blew a horn, long and loud. Then he walked around the tree and shook a pair of rattles. He was waking everyone at the camp, calling to them to join him. Women emerged from their huts, children peeked out the windows, and young teenagers came out of the community center. With all eyes on him, he stopped playing the instruments. He made an announcement, his booming voice overpowering the sound of Mariah's hysterical sobbing.

Christina and Dylan couldn't understand his language, but Christina recognized his gestures. The man pointed at Mariah and then at the prisoners. He was talking about them—about the invaders. He grabbed the severed, crispy testicle from the smoldering wood, sparks of fire spiraling to the ground. He held it over his head and wagged it at his people, as if to say: *this is how we punish trespassers and killers.*

Dylan asked, "What is he saying?"

"I'm not sure," Christina responded. "Maybe he's saying something like... like 'they deserve this.' He's talking about our punishment."

"But I didn't do anything. I swear, I didn't break any rules. I was–"

"I know, sweetie. This was... It's all a big misunderstanding. Just like the crash, this was all just one big accident. We didn't do anything wrong, but they don't know that."

"Why? Are they evil?"

"No. Well, maybe they're... I don't know how to explain it. Sometimes, good people do evil things. That's life, baby."

Christina gasped as someone reached into the cell. She swung at the arm, but she stopped before she could make physical contact.

"Wha–What is this?" she stuttered.

A girl reached into the cell, a bowl in her hand. The bowl was filled with açai berries, peach palm, and bananas. She grinned and nodded at Christina. A boy placed a bowl full of nuts on the ground beside them. He giggled as he ran off, blatantly excited. After Christina accepted the bowl of fruit, the girl joined the boy and they chatted. The kids were welcoming— gentle, sweet, genuine.

Christina looked at the leader. The leader smirked and gave her a nod, like a man buying a drink for a woman at a bar. She couldn't reject the gift. She had already eaten a piece of a human heart after all and she had to take care of Dylan. She ate the peach palm and shoved a few açai berries into Dylan's mouth.

She realized the tribespeople weren't

cannibalistic by law or nature. They didn't enjoy torturing people or consuming their flesh. But they accepted it as part of life. They weren't the savages shown in old exploitation films. Only some of the tribesmen found joy in the suffering.

Dylan's taste buds tingled with delight, but his stomach twisted and turned. After witnessing his father's torture, he didn't trust the tribe. Hunger had a way of persuading people, though. He ate some nuts and watched the tribespeople, vigilant.

Mouth full of fruit, Christina said, "Honey, if you want to survive... you have to do *everything* they tell you. Okay?" She swallowed the fruit with one loud *gulp.* She asked, "Do you understand me?"

"I-I understand. But I'm always a good boy, ma–ma'am. I listen and I, um... I... I behave. Everyone always told me that. Mom, dad, Ms. Hughes... I just want my mommy and daddy. I want Mariah back. I'm good, not bad. I swear."

"I know that. I know how you feel. But Mariah can't come back and it's because she didn't listen to them. Okay? If you listen to them, if you just follow my lead, I promise you'll see your mom as soon as we escape. You saw that drone, right? That means there's a rescue team nearby. We just have to wait for them. It's just a little longer. Please, *please,* listen to me."

Dylan looked up at the sky and thought about his mother. *Maybe she was flying that thing,* he thought, *she's my guardian angel, like she always said.* His eyes were drawn to Mariah, who was still held against the tree while the leader gave a speech to the tribe.

Dylan asked, "What about Mariah? Can we save her?"

"Mariah, she, um... she's making a sacrifice. Do you know what that means?"

Dylan shook his head.

Christina sighed, then she said, "Well, she's giving her life for us. She's going to buy us some time. That way, the rescue team can find us and you can be reunited with your mother."

Shocked, Dylan leaned away from her and said, "Giving her life? She's dying? They're going to kill her?!"

Christina grimaced and glanced over at the center of the camp. She spotted two men approaching the tree with rods of bamboo. Dylan tried to squirm away from her, screaming and weeping, but she grabbed him and held him close to her chest. She shushed him and rocked back-and-forth.

She said, "Don't look, don't listen. It'll be over soon."

***

Mariah shrieked as her ankles and shins were beaten with the bamboo rods. A symphony of thuds, thumps, cracks, and crunches echoed through the jungle. She tried to move her legs, but the men were too strong. She could only shimmy, her feet gliding across the mud. Her tibias *snapped* while her ankles cracked and popped.

She cried, "Stop! Stop! Oh God! Ow! Stop it!"

The beating went on for five uninterrupted minutes. By the end of the attack, the bamboo rods split her shin open vertically—from her knee to her ankle on her right leg. Her broken bone could be seen in the massive gash. Blood rolled down her leg and across her foot. Her other shin was painted with every tint of purple, a small crater near the center. A chunk of her flesh was chipped off.

"My legs," she said, out of breath. "I can't... stand. My legs... Please stop."

A man swung the bamboo rod at her chest. Mariah hunched forward and gasped, a string of drool falling from her mouth. Another man swung his bamboo rod at her, too. Her breasts jiggled with the impact. One after the other, the men smacked her breasts with the rods. Clusters of tiny, round red-and-purple dots formed across her chest—*petechiae.* The patches of petechiae grew larger with each blow.

The edge of one of the rods cut into her left breast. Blood leaked out of the cut. A bead hung from her erect nipple, like a fresh drop of breast milk. With another hit, the blood splattered across Mariah's chest, on the rod, and on the men. Her chest was beaten until her breasts were blue and swollen, nearly a cup size larger.

Mariah let out a long, ghastly groan. She drew short, rapid breaths and each breath was accompanied by a whistling sound, as if she were suffering from an asthma attack. Some of her ribs were shattered by the bamboo rods. Her breasts ached and her chest burned. She was carried over to the tree stump.

The women and children retreated to their huts. The happy kids went back to their homes, smiles twisted into frowns. The violence was distressing.

Dragging out each word, Mariah mumbled, "Pl– Please... I–I don't... want... to... die."

From the corner of the cell, Dylan sniveled and

shouted, "Please help her! Please!"

"I wish I could," Christina said as she hugged him tightly, tears gushing from her eyes. She covered one of his ears with one hand and pressed his face against her chest. She repeated, "Don't look, don't listen. Don't look, don't listen. Don't look, don't listen."

Mariah's head was placed on the tree stump, her chin and chest against the wood. A man sat on her back, pushing her body down and aggravating her battered breasts. He grabbed a fistful of her hair and gripped the nape of her neck, pinning her to the stump. Her bloody, bruised legs trembled violently. Even if she could knock the man off of her, she couldn't stand up. Her teeth grinded against each other because of the pressure on the back of her head and neck. She couldn't open her mouth.

Speaking through her clenched jaw, she said, "Please don't... hurt me... anymore. I'm... innocent."

The leader approached the stump with a sharp machete in his hand. As soon as she spotted the glint of sunshine on the blade, Mariah screamed and thrashed about. The young tribesman rode her like a bull, laughing at her reaction.

"Please, please, please," Mariah cried out. "Oh no, God, please don't do this. I–I'm young. I'm only twenty-two. I want to see my mom and my dad and my brother again. And my friends. I love my friends and family. Do you know love? Hmm? You know it, don't you? I–I'm a good person. I lo–love people. I love kids. I–I'm supposed to go back and–and become a teacher. I have so much to do. You understand? Please don't kill me. I'll do anything."

The leader stared at her with a deadpan expression. He pointed at her with the machete, then he tapped the blade against his chest and shook his head. The gesture translated to: *we must settle this, there's no way around it.*

Mariah yelled, "Please, mister, please! God, I don't want to die!"

From then on, those were her only words: *I don't want to die.* She repeated the sentence over and over, as if the repetitions would help her communicate with the tribespeople. They didn't understand her language, but they understood fear. Unfortunately for Mariah, terrorizing their enemies was their goal.

The leader tapped the edge of the blade against the top of Mariah's head—one, two, *three times*. He raised the machete over his head, all of his fingers wrapped around the handle.

Mucus pouring out of her nose and saliva spurting from her clenched teeth, Mariah screamed, "I don't want to die! I don't want to die! I don't want to–"

The leader swung the machete down. Mariah's screaming came to a sudden stop. The tribesmen stayed quiet, voices muffled by awe. The mothers pulled their children away from the windows while the teenagers lowered their heads and looked away. Christina dug her fingers into Dylan's scalp and shoulder, horrified. Dylan nearly yelped, but he knew it wasn't the time or place. He had to be strong.

Birds chirped, monkeys cried, and leaves rustled with the wind. The jungle continued to speak, unaffected by the human tragedy.

Mariah's head was chopped in half with one swing of the machete, from the top of her head to the region behind her chin. The front half of her skull fell forward, falling apart on the way down. The frontal bone rolled on the stump, like a bowl spinning on a kitchen counter. Her mandible, along with the severed half of her tongue, sat on the wood.

Her brain appeared to be throbbing while her optic nerves hung out of her head. Columns of blood shot out of her sliced brain. Her mouth was turned into a permanent hole, exposing her uvula, severed tongue, and remaining teeth. Her body twitched under the man, as if she were still fighting for life.

Bloody machete in hand, the leader stared into the jungle and shouted. It sounded like he was giving a warning to someone.

Do not harm my people, do not harm our land. Invaders will be punished.

Christina's eyes and mouth widened. A croaked escaped her mouth, flowing past her dry, chapped lips. She couldn't scream. She could only watch in horror.

The leader dug his fingers into the front half of Mariah's skull. With the machete, he sliced a piece of her brain off. Then, he shoved the brain into his mouth. Blood squirted out with each bite, dribbling across his chin and landing on the mud. He continued to yell at the jungle while waving the machete overhead—*a battle cry.*

Some of the other men joined him. They picked at her brain on both sides of her skull, tearing chunks of the organ with their fingers. They ate the brain—*raw.* The others didn't have the stomach for raw human organs. They lit the earth oven, then they cooked her brain and tongue. Some of the older men forced the teenagers to eat the cooked flesh.

One of the men ate an eyeball. Each bite—each *crunch*—filled his mouth with bloody vitreous. The metallic taste of the blood overwhelmed the other flavors in his mouth. He chewed on it for a few minutes, as if he had stuck an entire pack of gum into his mouth. Then, he slurped and sucked on his fingers. It was a treat to him.

A cool breeze wafted the stench of cooked organs into the cell. Dylan peeked over at the stump as he caught a whiff of the death. Goops of purple paste fell out of his mouth as he vomited the açai berries. He fainted in Christina's arms, his limp head falling back over her forearm. He kept hacking and retching, though. He was choking on his own puke.

Christina finally snapped out of her fear-induced trance. She lifted Dylan's head and shoved her fingers into his mouth, pulling the rest of the puke out. She shook him gently, trying to awaken him. She believed he was better off unconscious, but she was afraid of being alone with the tribespeople. A young, timid boy couldn't protect her, but his presence would at least bring her some comfort.

She looked up at the ceiling of the cell and yelled, "Help us! Please, God! We're out of time!"

Chapter Thirteen

The Border

Nathan walked into a creek, the water sparkling around him with a ray of sunshine. The clear water reached his waist, fish swimming past him. He took a sip of water from his cupped hands, then he scrubbed the mud off his face and neck. But he stopped as he caught a glimpse of his reflection on the water.

Mud stained his skin, but, in his reflection, the brown streaks looked red. He saw himself covered in blood—*Michael's blood, Cole's blood, everyone's blood.* He scoured himself, scratching his arms and neck. He even rubbed rocks against his knuckles. Yet, through the rippling water, he still saw nothing but blood on his flesh.

He muttered, "I fucked up, guys. I tried to find them, but it's like a goddamn maze out here. Everything looks the same. And those bastards are so damn fast. I couldn't keep track of them. I'm a coward and a failure."

He stopped scrubbing his knuckles. He crouched slowly, submerging himself in the creek. Within seconds, the water reached his shoulders. He glued his eyes to a tree. He didn't want to think about the other passengers or his family. His survivor's guilt returned, reminding him of the plane crash and the massacre at the tribe's camp. For some reason, perhaps luck or some divine intervention, he was spared and given a second and *third* chance.

But he wished he died during the crash. Dying in a fiery explosion or falling to his death didn't seem so bad compared to being eaten alive by ants, beaten with branches, mutilated, and scalped.

I'm a coward, he thought. *I don't deserve to go back to my family. Holly could never love a man like me. And what will they tell Kyle? That I let everyone die? That I ran away and abandoned them?*

As the water caressed his chin, a voice emerged from beyond the rocks to his left. The sound of running, clashing water drowned it out, but he heard a few words. He stood up, his soaked clothes hanging heavy from his body. He clambered up the rocks until he reached the edge of a stone. He found the creek led to a series of cascades. A few meters below, the creek continued cutting through the jungle.

Francisco Silva, an anthropologist, stood in the creek, water splashing against his dark brown pants. He wore a khaki button-up shirt with the sleeves folded up. His large backpack was securely strapped onto him. A leaf was stuck in his curly brown hair. His skin was tanned, but he didn't resemble the tribespeople. He looked like an explorer from an action movie—Indiana Jones or Lara Croft.

He stood in a half-squat, his arms raised with his fingers pointed away from himself, as if he were trying to tame a wild animal.

"No queremos problemas," he said in Spanish. "Solo queremos hablar."

It translated to: *we don't want any problems, we only want to talk.* Nathan gasped as he noticed the tribe's scouts on the other side of the creek. One man stood near the water, a spear in his right hand with the blade aiming skyward. He performed an unusual gesture. He held his free hand close to his mouth, blew into it, and then he waved it at the man, as if he were blowing a kiss. Taking cover behind a stone, another tribesman stood on a slope behind him with his bow drawn. The third tribesman was crouched on a branch, aiming at the anthropologist from above. They were ready to kill him.

In Brazilian Portuguese, Francisco said, "Escute-me, cavalheiros. Nós viemos em paz. Por–"

An arrow zoomed past him from above. A wave of water burst upward and hit his arm while the arrow struck the bottom of the creek with incredible force. His words had translated to: *listen to me, gentlemen. We come in peace.* The arrow interrupted him before he could say 'please.' The tribespeople weren't there for peace talks.

"Perdão!" Francisco shouted as he staggered back. "Perdão!"

Pardon! Pardon!

Behind Francisco, a group of men emerged from the jungle, wearing camouflage uniforms and armed with IMBEL IA2 assault rifles. The men formed a platoon of soldiers. They aimed their weapons at the tribesmen, fingers on their triggers, and they shouted in Brazilian Portuguese.

Francisco turned towards the men, then he glanced back at the tribesmen. *A massacre*—his gut told him he was about to witness a massacre if he didn't intervene.

In Portuguese, he said, "Certo, se acalme, se acalme." In Spanish, he said, "Vamos a calmarnos.

Bueno?"

His message boiled down to: *okay, let's calm down.* Yet, the scouts and the soldiers kept aiming at each other.

The man with the spear stepped forward. He raised the spear over his shoulder and crouched, ready to throw it at the first sign of trouble. He nodded at Francisco and he said something. Nathan couldn't hear his words, he didn't understand his language anyway, but he recognized the anger in the man's scowl—the fire raging in his eyes.

Francisco stood there and listened. His eyes glowed with curiosity, like a passionate student's. He wanted to ask a million questions, but he wasn't there as an anthropologist. He was recruited by the army to serve as a translator on a special mission. He exchanged a few words with the tribesman. The conversation ended with a smile and nod from Francisco while the tribesman lowered his spear. Francisco returned to the soldiers near the creek.

Nathan looked to his left, then to his right. He was surrounded by deadly forces—a group of murderous tribesmen and a troop of trigger-happy soldiers. He had one question for himself: *do I want to get shot with arrows or bullets?* He already knew enough about the tribe, so he decided to spy on the soldiers. He wiggled across the rocks until he reached dry land. He crawled slowly down a hill, shielded by the thick foliage and bushes.

He stopped, as still as a sculpture.

"These are good men in a bad place, Cardoso."

He heard those words—*in English*. He raised his head until he could peek over a bush. He spotted

Francisco speaking to a hardened, grizzled soldier. The soldier was in his fifties, but he was healthy and lethal. His cold, distant eyes told stories of loss, extreme violence, and personal tragedy. He lived a difficult life, but he persevered for himself, his family, his religion, and his country. His name was Davi Cardoso, and he was the leader of the operation.

Matching Francisco's thick accent, Davi said, "There are always good men in bad places, Mr. Silva. That is not our concern. We are conducting a search-and-rescue mission. We want passage. Did you explain that to these 'gentlemen?' Could you communicate with them?"

"We shared a few words, yes. I told them about the plane crash and the rescue mission, but… they don't trust you."

"Me?"

Francisco responded, "You and your soldiers. They say you are responsible for countless murders in the region. You and the traffickers and the deforesters have been wiping out the tribes of the Amazon and destroying their homes. You are destroying this land." He took a step back as he noticed Davi's glare. He stuttered, "Tha–That's what they told me. Those were their words, sir."

"They do not speak the truth, Mr. Silva. My soldiers do not enter this jungle without reason, and that reason has never been to commit acts of genocide. *However,* if we find it necessary to rescue the survivors of that crash, lethal force has been authorized. You have to remember: *El Presidente* doesn't care very much for these people. He does not have a soft spot for them. My opinion about them doesn't matter. I will find those survivors, one way or another. Now, please, ask them again. And let them know: there is only one correct answer."

Francisco reluctantly returned to the creek. He spoke to the tribesman in Spanish and Brazilian Portuguese. He tried to speak their language, too. Nathan figured Francisco and Davi spoke English during their conversation so the tribesmen wouldn't understand them. He crawled backwards, his eyes on the soldiers. *Lethal force has been authorized*—Davi's message sent chills down his spine. He wondered if they were concerned about collateral damage. He couldn't take the risk.

Not yet.

As Nathan made his way up the hill, Francisco screamed at the top of his lungs. A gunshot echoed through the woods, quickly followed by a burst of gunfire—*and then another.* Nathan reached the stones at the top of the cascades. He lay flat on a large stone, water splashing against his feet, and he watched the encounter from above.

An arrow protruded from Francisco's shoulder. Blood soaked his shirt and stained his neck. A soldier dragged him out of the creek. Before they could find cover, an arrow struck Francisco's thigh, barely missing his femoral artery by an inch. The soldiers shot at the scouts, their bullets mowing down bushes, shredding through the foliage, and penetrating the tree trunks.

The archer on the branch was hit with three bullets. One bullet went straight through his heart and exited through his back. The second round became stuck in his pectoral muscle. The last round went through his collarbone and exited through his trapezius. He was dead before he hit the ground, leaves spiraling down to his corpse like cherry blossoms during the springtime.

The other archer hid between a large stone and a thick tree trunk. He shot arrows at the soldiers while bullets ricocheted off the stone and cracked the trunk beside him. Wood chips hit his face and landed in his eyes, negatively affecting his accuracy, but he kept shooting arrows at them. He was buying time—nothing more, nothing less. He couldn't stand up against a small army of well-equipped soldiers.

Nathan spotted the tribesman with the spear running into the jungle. The man was yelling, one hand on his back. He connected the pieces: he was running back to the camp to inform the others of the incursion.

"What do I do? What do I do?" Nathan whispered, his voice masked by the gunfire. "The soldiers, they're here to rescue us. I can run over there and they'll take care of me, right? I might get shot if I scare them, but they wouldn't kill me on purpose. No, I'd be safe. I can end this right now."

He glanced over at the jungle to his left. He pictured the survivors in the cell—nude, muddy, *bloody.* He heard their screaming in his head. He felt their panic, their fear, and their pain. He believed he owed them his personal help.

He said, "They won't help me, even if I beg. I need to do this on my own, but... maybe I can use them. They'll be my distraction. They're coming here, aren't they? So I can go back and save the rest of 'em. Yeah, this is my chance to do the right thing." He ran into the jungle and retraced his steps. Pushing through the bushes and tripping over the foliage, he said, "For Cole, for Michael, for everyone."

Chapter Fourteen

Pau de Arara

"You can't do this to me! I listened to you! I ate everything!" Christina shouted. "I'm begging you! I don't want to die! Not like this! I'll... I'll... I'll fuck you! You can fuck me! Don't do this!"

Christina cried hysterically, but she didn't produce any tears. She was dehydrated, leaving her tear ducts as dry as dust. She gritted her teeth so hard that a loud, clear *cracking* sound escaped her mouth. Her face, neck, and chest reddened, veins sticking out in webs, splintering off in every direction like the jungle's rivers.

A group of men carried her to the center of the camp where Christina's body was slumped over the stump. Flies buzzed around the severed pieces of her skull. A fly landed on the base of her tongue, then it skittered past her uvula and entered her throat. Dried, dark blood stained the stump and the surrounding ground.

Christina screamed as two of the men released her arms. The other two tightened their grips on her legs. Her upper body fell, the back of her head hitting the ground within two seconds. Her screaming stopped, replaced by a long, slow groan. Pain pulsated from the back of her head and her neck ached. She wasn't knocked out by the blow, but she felt drowsy.

"Wha–What are you doing to me?" she whispered as the men lifted her from the ground again. "I–I don't... want to die. Let's... talk."

"Let her go!" Dylan shouted from the cell. "Hey! Please! Don't hurt my friend!"

"No, Dy–Dylan... honey... don't fight them," Christina said softly, barely audible. "Just... Just turn around and don't look."

A sturdy pole was placed under her knees. Her arms were pulled forward and then up towards her knees, causing her to bend forward. Her wrists and ankles were tied together with twine around the pole. The men carried the pole on their shoulders, leaving her body hanging about a meter above the ground like a human chandelier. She swung back and forth, locks of hair dangling under her.

It was the perfect parrot's perch—*the Pau De Arara.* The method of torture had been used for generations in the region. The tribespeople learned it from their invaders, and they mastered it.

The joint pain came first. The burning pain ran from her wrists to her elbows and her ankles to her knees. She felt like her bones were dislocating, popping and crunching. The pain flowed slowly into her thighs and biceps, like drops of acid dripping into her veins from an IV—slow and fiery. Her limbs went numb. The prickling sensation reminded her of ants, and ants reminded her of Michael, and Michael reminded her of large, carnivorous ants.

Swinging from the parrot's perch, she shook her head and cried, "Oh, please! It hurts so bad! It burns so much!" Drawing hoarse, shallow breaths between each word, she said, "Oh... my... God... Please..."

After three minutes, the pain reached her head. She swore the throbbing headache caused her skull to vibrate. Her brain was pounding at her skull, as if the organ had taken on a life of its own and it wanted to escape its prison. *No, not me, I don't want to be chopped in half and eaten,* her brain would say, *not today.* The veins on her forehead grew larger while her skin took on the brightest shade of red. It looked like blood was smeared on her face and chest—blood that couldn't be washed off.

"My–My head... It–It's going to–to explode..."

The men ignored her. They pulled Dylan out of the cell, dragging him across the mud on his back.

Dylan swung at them and shouted, "No! No! I didn't do nothin'! I was good! I was–"

He stopped as he spotted Mariah's dead body over the stump. He tried not to look earlier. Christina had warned him about the extreme violence and its effects on his brain. He believed her, too. The stench—a scent comprised of rotting meat, old blood, and feces—attracted him to the corpse. He saw the crap and urine on her thighs. He stared at her open skull, a blank expression on his face. His systems shut down—*everything* shut down. He was an empty shell, a body without a soul.

Children weren't meant to see the type of carnage that occurred in the rainforest after the crash. It wasn't natural.

His eyes fell shut as he faded away, limp and unconscious. The leader kicked the corpse off the stump and pointed at it, gesturing his demands. They lifted Dylan from the ground, then they laid his body down on the stump spread-eagled. Chunks of brain were crushed under his back, like gum under a shoe.

Christina's eyelids twitched as she watched the group. A bank of fog swept over her eyes and clouded her vision, everything was upside down, but her view of Dylan was clear. He was surrounded by three tribesmen, then four, and then five. They examined his nude body, but not in a sexual way. Like construction workers demolishing a building, they searched for the best way to deconstruct his body.

Christina said, "Don't hurt him. Hurt me, fuck me, eat me. Do whatever you want to me, but don't touch him. You, um... You're better than that, aren't you? I've seen your kids. They're *good* kids so they must have *good* parents, right? Let him go and walk away while you still have your pride. Please, don't hurt this child because of an accident. Even if you don't believe us, don't hurt him for someone else's sins."

The leader approached the stump with a hatchet. He tapped the blade against Dylan's shins gently. He only cut him once. He nicked him, that was all.

"Don't do it. Please don't hurt him," Christina begged.

He tapped the boy's kneecaps and thighs. He swung down at his crotch, but he stopped before he could mutilate him. He grinned at Christina.

"No, no, no, no, no," Christina said rapidly. "You– You can't do this to him. Please! Listen to me, goddammit!"

The leader slid the blade up Dylan's stomach. He stopped at his chest, right above his sternum. He raised the hatchet over his head, then he swung down at Dylan.

Christina closed her eyes before the hatchet hit the boy's chest. She heard his sudden gasp and the *crunch* of his bones. She could hear the blood *squirting* out of his chest. Then, Dylan moaned as he writhed in pain. The men held him down as the leader swung the hatchet at him again. He broke through the sternum and ruptured his heart. Dylan didn't make another sound.

"You monsters!" Christina yelled, eyes clenched shut. "He was a boy! He didn't deserve this! Why would you... do something like this? We're innocent. We didn't do anything to you. He was... Oh God, he was just a damn kid!"

She felt someone's palms on the sides of her head. Then, she felt his long, spindly fingers crawling onto her cheeks. *He's going for my eyes,* she thought. She squeezed her eyes shut as tightly as possible, shook her head frantically, and shrieked. The man yelled at her while trying to pry her eyes open.

Christina cried, "No! Please! Why?! Oh my God! I don't want to see it! You bastards! You–"

She squealed in pain as the man forced his finger into her left eye socket. Her eye hemorrhaged as his sharp, dirty fingernail cut into it. A droplet of blood oozed out and rolled down her forehead. The pain caused her to panic, so she unintentionally opened her other eye. The man placed his fingers on her eyelids, prying them open.

She could barely see a thing from her bloody eye. The left side of her vision was red and unfocused. But she saw clearly through her right eye. Dylan lay on the stump. His torso was open down the middle, ribs sticking out of his chest and pointing away from his body. His ruptured heart and his lungs were removed.

A group of men huddled around the earth oven and cooked the organs.

Hands drenched in blood, the leader sawed his liver out and handed it to another man. The man went over to the earth oven, ready for his turn to cook. The leader moved on to Dylan's stomach. He cut off the gallbladder and he sliced into his pancreas while attempting to cut out his stomach. Thick green fluid, tainted with clouds of blood, came out of a laceration on his stomach. They paid it no mind.

Christina was awed by the savagery. The shock temporarily relieved the pain in her left eye. The tribespeople spoke to each other, chatting as if they were carving a turkey during a Thanksgiving dinner, but she didn't hear a word. Nature didn't speak to her, either. The world stopped moving to mourn the death of an innocent child.

She stuttered, "Dy–Dylan, hon–honey. Please... wake up. Run away from all of... *this*. Get up and run, sweetie. You–You're a kid. You're supposed to run and have fun. Come on, please get up." She puffed and snorted and coughed, hysterical. She glared at the men, her lips trembling with anger, and she said, "Kill me. If you don't, if I get free, I promise you'll pay for this. I'll cut you into little pieces and I'll eat *all* of you. It will be like you never existed. You'll be–"

She gritted her teeth, growled in pain, and dropped an inch as one of her ankles *popped.* Her ankle was dislocated, bones and ligaments damaged beyond repair. The rod groaned with the pressure of her weight. The surrounding men laughed at her, amused by her suffering. Dylan's stomach in his hand, blood and stomach fluid dripping down to the ground, the leader chuckled and wagged his finger at her. Then he bit into the organ. *Hmm*—the sound of satisfaction seeped past his bloody lips.

"You... You understand me, don't you? You speak English, right?" Christina asked weakly. "You... monsters. You're... not... going to–"

She fell unconscious mid-sentence, unable to withstand the pain. She dropped another inch as her wrists cracked. Her hands almost slipped out of the twine. The man to her left, the rod over his shoulder, reached over and tightened the knots. The twine sliced into her skin. Her hands and feet turned blue. Balancing himself on one foot, the other man hit the back of her head with his knee, trying to awaken her from her slumber.

The men stopped upon hearing a faint shout. Some of the families emerged from their huts, curious. They gazed into the jungle and whispered amongst themselves. The shouting grew louder. The leader reached for a spear, but he stopped before he could touch the weapon. He heard a word. It was his tribe's language. Then he recognized the voice. It was one of the scouts.

A young man stumbled out of the jungle, his spear falling to the ground with him. He gasped as he writhed about on the mud, twisting and turning. His lower back, buttocks, and legs were covered in blood. The cloth around his waist was soaked, too. Pints of blood had poured out of a tiny hole on his back—*a gunshot wound*. He was shot while retreating. The bullet was trapped in his stomach.

The leader flipped him over and held him in his

arms. He called for water and medicine—*help!* His face scrunched up, the scout told him about the army at the creek and the shootout. A group of women approached with buckets of water, but it was too late. The young man passed away in his arms, bloody saliva foaming out of his mouth.

The tribe shared a moment of silence. The leader walked to the center of the camp, staring at his steady, bloody hands. He had been there before, but he needed a second to think. He glanced around, running his eyes over the tribespeople and their homes. They looked back at him, waiting for his orders. The women and children looked sad and frightened while the men appeared eager and determined. They knew what was coming.

The leader raised a spear over his head and screamed. The men grabbed weapons from the ground, the huts, and the community center—bows and arrows, knives, spears, machetes, hatchets, and blowguns and shotguns. They chanted and ran into the jungle, ready for war. The women stayed at the camp with the children under thirteen years old. Two young men—fifteen and sixteen years old—stayed behind to carry the parrot's perch. Christina's torture saw no end.

Chapter Fifteen

The Fight for Redemption

Nathan slid across the mud on his stomach. He leaned back against a tree, hid under a bush, and draped some vines over his shoulders. The tribespeople ran past him and headed in the opposite direction. One, two, three, four, five—he couldn't count them all, but he figured there were at least a dozen of them stampeding through the woods.

In a sense, he was happy to see them. He had lost track of the scout during his trek through the jungle. He became confused and disoriented. Every tree, every bush, and every vine looked the same. But he recognized the tribesmen. Although they closely resembled each other, he couldn't forget those killers. The torture was engraved in his mind—*a permanent memory.*

After a minute, the last tribesman vanished behind a tree. A minute after that, their chanting faded away.

Nathan struggled to his feet. He followed their footprints to retrace their steps, constantly glancing over his shoulder. To his utter relief, he didn't see or hear anyone. The relief was only temporary, though. The silence was deafening. He thought about the camp and the other survivors—about the screaming, the sobbing, *the begging.* Now, hours later, he heard nothing in the area.

"Mariah, Dylan," he whispered. "Oh my God, no. Please don't let it be true. They're okay, they're safe.

I'm not late. I can save them. It's not over yet."

He lurched through a tall bush, then he fell to his knees. He found himself at the tribe's camp. He had been there before, close enough at least, but it looked like an entirely different camp. The differences were jarring, night-and-day. Kids played near the outskirts of the camp, young teenagers gathered berries at the garden, and women cooked at the community center.

It was peaceful.

Nathan's eyes were drawn to the tree stump. He spotted Dylan's dissected body. It looked as if he had exploded from within. His heart, lungs, and liver burned in the earth oven. The ground around the stump was bestrewn with his intestines. His skin was pale, as white as milk, and his lips were blue. The nine-year-old boy was butchered.

Mariah was difficult to identify due to her missing face, but he recognized her curly hair and curvy figure. He was disgusted by her horrific death.

Nathan staggered as he retched and coughed. His vision dimmed and cleared—dimmed and cleared, *dimmed and cleared.* He grabbed a fistful of hair in each hand and tugged on his head, furious and saddened by the death. He blamed himself for the carnage. He carried their coffins on his back. He thought: *what did they do to deserve this? Why did they slaughter all of them? How could they kill a child?*

He stopped tugging and shaking as he spotted a human figure from the corner of his eye. Two young men stood near the edge of the camp to his right, carrying the parrot's perch on their shoulders. Between them, Christina's body hung from the pole. She was conscious, watching him with her only good eye. She couldn't believe it, but it made sense. She remembered their conversation in the cell, the one about the survivor who got away. She wanted to say: *you must be Nathan.* But the surprise left her speechless.

The teenagers looked at each other, then at Christina, and then at Nathan. They didn't know how to react to the intrusion. They didn't participate in the torture, they never fought against the invaders.

Christina said, "Kill them... or they'll kill you."

One of the teenagers raised his hand to Nathan. He stuttered in a different language, so Nathan didn't understand his words. Fear was a universal language, though. He was asking for time and begging for mercy: *please don't hurt us, wait until our parents come home, we can talk about this.* The time for talk had ended when Michael's torture began.

Nathan grabbed a football-sized stone from the ground. It weighed at least five pounds. One of the teenagers stepped back and the other young man took a step to his left, leaving the parrot's perch unbalanced. Nathan walked forward, his shoulders rising with each heavy breath. His fury numbed the pain in his chest. The teenagers took a few more steps back, then they tumbled. Christina hit the muddy ground head-first.

She shouted, "Don't let them kill you! Fight!"

Nathan pounced on the fifteen-year-old, mounting him at the waist. Blinded by his rage, he swung the stone down at his face. The rough, jagged-edge of the stone ripped his left temple open. The young man was instantly knocked unconscious. He hit him again.

He tore a chunk of skin off his cheek, exposing the bone underneath. He hit him a third time. The teenager's nose was shattered. His left nostril collapsed while blood poured out of the right nostril like a miniature tsunami. His nasal septum was pushed an inch to the right.

The other teenager tackled him while screaming at him. He mounted him in an awkward position, one knee under his left armpit and the other over his right shoulder. He swung down at him with the bottom of his fists, striking his face, shoulder, and chest. One of the blows sliced Nathan's bottom lip, another caused a minor nosebleed. The punches hurt, but the teenager wasn't very strong. Without a weapon, he couldn't neutralize Nathan. Murder was his only option. He wrapped his hands around his neck and attempted to strangle him.

Nathan fought back as soon as he felt the teenager's thumbs digging into his throat. He hit him with a barrage of hooks from below—left, right, left, *right.* By the fourth punch, blood was already leaking out of the teenager's lips. Blood cascaded from his gums and painted his teeth red. The teenager pulled his head back as far as humanly possible. He glanced over at his fellow guard and called out to him: *help!* There was no response. His peer was knocked out cold. So, he looked over at the huts and yelled.

Meanwhile, Christina tried to free herself from the parrot's perch. The wounds on her wrists and ankles widened. The sight of her own blood made her woozy, but redemption was her only concern. She had to help Nathan to help herself. One of her hands slipped out the twine. Her wrist was slit open horizontally, her severed veins visible in the wide gash. A twitchy grin on her face, hope glimmering in her eyes, she began yanking on the knots to release herself.

The rest of the tribespeople gathered around them. They weren't violent people. They didn't enjoy the torture or murder. Savagery wasn't in their genetics. They lived peacefully before the invaders arrived—traffickers, deforesters, mercenaries. When violence knocked on their door, they were forced to respond with violence. They couldn't harm Nathan or Christina. They shouted and beckoned at the teenager, saying something along the lines: *get off of him and run! Stop fighting! It's over!*

But Nathan grabbed the teenager's forearms and stopped him from running. He sat up and thrust his head at him. *Thud!*—the sound of the headbutt, like a melon hitting the floor, echoed through the camp. The young man's chin was split vertically down the middle. They fell away from each other, dazed by the collision. They squirmed on the ground, struggling to find their bearings.

Christina untied the last knot. She frowned as she stretched. Her entire body ached and itched. The tingling sensation in her limbs was replaced with a burning pain. Beneath her, the mud fused with her blood, creating a patch of rust-colored sludge. She crawled towards the surrounding group of men and children. The tribespeople staggered away, terrified. She grabbed a knife from the ground near the crownless tree trunk, then she made her way back to the parrot's perch.

Eyes full of tears, the tribeswomen called out to her: *please don't, it's over, we're sorry.* They asked her to spare their lives, but, at heart, they felt like they deserved it. Guilt haunted them, too.

Christina crawled onto the unconscious teenager's chest. She stared at his broken, bloodied face. He contributed to the torture by allowing it to occur and agreeing to carry the parrot's perch, but he was innocent. She considered sparing him, but then she heard the buzzing flies. Like roadkill on a Texas road in the summer, a swarm of flies flew around the corpses of Dylan and Mariah.

They were innocent, too, she told herself. *I followed their orders and they still tortured me. There are no rules. If we turn our backs on them, they'll stab us, they'll kill us, and they'll eat us.*

She gripped the knife with both hands, held it over her head with the blade aiming down, and whispered, "I'm sorry."

She thrust the knife at him. The flint blade penetrated the center of his throat. His right eye flickered open and a squeaky sound came out of his mouth. She wiggled the blade inside of his throat. Blood jetted out as the wound widened—one, two, *three squirts.* He reached for her arm, slow and weak. His fingers slid off the mud and blood on her forearm. His arms fell to his sides.

Christina placed more pressure on the handle, pushing the entire three-inch blade into his neck, then she yanked the knife out. Hot blood erupted from his throat in short bursts. Then the blood flooded his mouth and frothed on his lips. He shook and grunted as he clung to life.

Christina cried, "Just die already!"

She forced her thumb, index, and middle fingers into the wound on his throat. She grabbed a sturdy piece of flesh. *A vein? A muscle?*–she thought. She pulled and *she pulled* until his larynx protruded from his neck, like a prolapsing anus. The pain was unbearable. A whistling sound came out of *somewhere,* but she didn't know where. He passed away, but he kept shaking for thirty seconds.

Christina rolled onto her back beside him. He covered her mouth and sobbed as she stared up at the sky. She questioned herself: *for redemption or for vengeance?*

As they stood up, the other teenager stabbed the small of Nathan's back with an arrow. Screaming in pain, Nathan turned around and hit the teenager's head with his elbow.

He pulled the arrow out of his back and shouted, "Fuck! Goddammit!"

The teenager ran towards him with another arrow. In a knee-jerk reaction, Nathan kicked him in the crotch, his shin crushing his genitals. The teenager crossed his legs and fell to his knees. He was neutralized by the attack. It would take him at least an hour to fully recover from such a vicious blow. An hour was enough time to escape. But Nathan kept hearing Christina's words in his head: *kill them or they'll kill you.* He had witnessed the tribe's brutality. He couldn't trust them.

He tackled the teenager and mounted his waist. He stabbed him repeatedly with the arrow. First, he targeted his chest. His pectoral muscles were riddled with stab wounds, about one-inch long and one-inch deep. There were fourteen stab wounds across his chest. The cuts were painful, but they weren't life-threatening. The teenager panicked after Nathan stabbed him in the neck five times. He felt his jugular *burst,* like a knuckle popping in his hand. He breathed deeply through his nose and tried to stop the bleeding with his palm.

Nathan stabbed his face. The arrowhead went through his cheek and slid into his mouth. The wound widened when he pulled the arrow out. It looked like he was shot through the cheek. He stabbed him again. The arrowhead ruptured his left eye. The third and fourth stabs mutilated his nose. Then, the arrow snapped in his hand as he stabbed the teenager's forehead. By then, the young guard was already dead. The shock and loss of blood killed him.

Nathan stood up, teetering around with blood splattered on his arms and face. The tribespeople surrounded them, horror written on their faces. He saw something different, though. He saw the cannibals from the worst exploitation films ever made, he saw savages with a taste for blood. He picked up a machete and swung it at them, trying to keep them at bay. But, none of them approached him. They were just as scared of him as he was of them.

He shouted, "You bastards! You see what you made me do?! You think I wanted to do that?! Fuck! Damn it! Why couldn't you leave us alone? We survived a fuckin' plane crash for crying out loud. That's all. We didn't do anything to you. We... We were... What... Did..." He turned into a blubbering mess. He swung the machete to his left and barked, "Stay back! Don't come any closer! I'll kill you, too! I mean it!"

He pointed the machete at a boy with a bowl-cut hairdo. The child didn't move an inch—before, during, and after Nathan's speech.

"You have to go," Christina said weakly. "Get out of here... before the others come back."

Watching the tribespeople with a set of vigilant eyes, Nathan responded, "They're not coming back. They went to the creek. They're going to fight against an army of soldiers, and they're going to lose. The rescue team is on its way, I'm positive about that, but I think we should start moving towards them now. We have to get the hell out of here. Today!"

"The creek? What creek?"

"I don't know. *A* creek. Don't worry, I know how to get there."

"Sol–Soldiers?"

"Guys with guns, okay?" Nathan said, growing frustrated by the questions. He knelt down beside her with the machete pointed at the tribe. He said, "We have to go."

"I can't."

"You can. I'll help you."

Christina pushed his arm away and said, "No, I can't. Go on without me. I'll, um... I'll make sure none of them follow you."

"Are you kidding me? Look, I don't know you, but I'm not leaving you behind. I watched these people die. Michael, Cole... I didn't know them very long, but they took care of me. They were good people and they didn't deserve *that*. That *boy* didn't deserve *that*. I already have to live with their deaths on my conscience, I'm not going to live with yours. I'm getting you out of here."

He tossed her arm over his shoulder, then he grabbed her waist and helped her to her feet. Her legs wobbled due to her fractured, lacerated ankles.

She cried, "Just leave me. I'm dead weight. Please, I don't deserve to live."

"You deserve better than this. Hold onto me, I'm getting us out of here."

Christina continued mumbling: *leave me, I deserve to die, I didn't help them, I ate human flesh.* Nathan didn't hear a word. He was busy swinging the machete at the tribespeople to keep them away. The remaining tribespeople weren't eager to follow them. Women covered the bodies of the dead teenagers with blankets. The community grieved for their dead tribemates, devastated by their loss.

Chapter Sixteen

The Great Escape

Nathan led Christina through the jungle, ducking under vines, running through bushes, and juking past snakes and other wild animals. Christina hobbled behind him, blood squirting out of her ankles with each step. He kept his arm around her throughout their journey, determined to save at least *one* person. He avoided the tribe's path, though, in case they returned after their inevitable defeat at the creek.

The long way, go around, take the long way, go around them, he told himself over and over.

They winced and crouched behind a bush upon hearing a rapid succession of gunshots. In the maze of trees, a man screamed. It was a shout of pain—of fear, *of desperation.* After a minute, there was another gunshot. The screaming stopped before the gunshot's echoes ended. The sound of arrows *whizzing* between the trees followed. Another man shouted in pain.

"Fui ferido!" he yelled.

I'm hit!

Nathan peeked over the bush. He saw two tribesmen dragging a dead comrade through the jungle. An archer sat on a branch above them, shooting arrows and dodging gunfire. Another tribesman, tall and burly, lobbed spears at the army from a hill. One of the spears impaled a soldier, skewering him through the stomach.

The soldiers found cover behind trees and stones. They shot at the tribe with their assault rifles, shotguns, and pistols. Two soldiers provided suppressing fire, allowing the others to move up. The tribesman with the spears was flanked by three soldiers. In less than fifteen seconds, twenty bullets from two IMBEL IA2 rifles riddled his body—ten in the torso, four in the left arm, two in the left leg, and four in the head.

One bullet entered his left cheek and exited through the other, leaving a massive exit wound on the right side of his face. The second round went through his left cheekbone and became trapped behind his nose. The third and fourth bullets penetrated his left temple. He rolled down a hill, two spears following him down into a ditch.

Laying on her side, Christina asked, "What are you waiting for?" Nathan didn't respond. Christina nudged his leg with her elbow and said, "Go, save yourself."

"What?" Nathan asked, observing the massacre with narrowed eyes.

"Go to them. They'll protect you. They'll... They'll take you out of this hell."

Nathan finally looked at her. He glanced over at the soldiers. One of them shot a spider monkey out of a tree with pinpoint precision. They killed without thinking twice—hell, they didn't think once about it. It was their specialty. They were trained to kill and groomed to follow orders. He reached for the machete, which he shoved between his belt and his waistband.

"I don't think it's safe for anyone right now,"

Nathan said. "They're shooting on sight, you see? If they see us, if we startle 'em, they might shoot us. We should just wait until they find us. That way, we can surrender and they won't–"

He held his hands over his ears and closed his eyes as a burst of gunfire interrupted him. The gunshots were louder than the others. The shooter was close.

Christina said, "Hey. *Hey.*"

Nathan opened his eyes. Another burst of gunfire echoed through the jungle, but he didn't hear it. He gazed into Christina's eyes—blue eyes with specks of glittering gold. She was smiling, but she wasn't nervous or scared. It was a smile of acceptance.

Nathan stuttered, "Wha–What's wrong?"

"Nothing. Nothing at all. Listen, I think you're going to make it out of here. Maybe we both can, but if we don't... *if we don't,* I want you to remember something for me. Okay?"

"What is it?"

"*My name.* My name is Christina Hernandez. I'm a flight attendant from Los Angeles, California. My husband's name is Carlos and my daughter... my princess' name is Isabella. If I don't make it, tell them that I died peacefully, okay? Tell them... Tell them you found my body strapped to a seat unharmed. I died from a heart attack, right? *Right?*"

"Ri–Right."

"Good, good. Give them peace. Don't tell them about what happened at that camp. Don't let them know about their suffering. It will scar them for life. It's better if it's just forgotten."

Nathan asked, "Why are you talking like that? Like

you're going to die? We just have to wait here and–"

"We can't wait. If we wait, the tribe might find us. If they don't kill us, we'll die during the shootout because they *will* cause a big scene. If we startle these soldiers like you said, then they might kill us anyway. I have to do something."

Nathan shook his head and asked, "What the hell are you saying?"

"I'm going to surrender. If they don't kill me, then you can come out and we'll leave this jungle once and for all. If they shoot... you run and find the real rescue team. Americans, the UN, the Red Cross, anyone who doesn't already have their finger on the trigger. And don't forget what I said."

Nathan saw the sincerity in Christina's eyes. She was serious about her plan. He couldn't argue with her, either. One wrong move and hundreds of bullets would shred them like cheese.

He said, "Christina, Carlos, Isabella, heart attack. I've got it. Don't die out there. Don't make me remember that."

"Let's hope you won't have to. Thank you, hun."

Christina leaned against a tree and pulled herself up to her feet. She winked at Nathan, a confident smile stretching across her face. Then she limped forward with her hands over her head.

She said, "Don't shoot! I'm Ameri–"

A hail of bullets struck her. From less than five meters away, a soldier shot her with a shotgun. The gunshot severed her right arm at the elbow. The arm fell to the ground beside her bloody foot. Rifle rounds hit the rest of her body from several angles, making her dance—*a Harlem Shake.* One of her breasts burst, a piece of her intestines popped out of a large wound on her abdomen, and her arms and legs were hit multiple times. One of her legs snapped back at the knee, hanging onto the rest of her limb by some exposed tendons and ligaments.

The top-right quadrant of her head exploded, shards of bone and bits of brain splattering on the bush behind her. She was dead a few gunshots before that, though.

"Oh fuck!" Nathan yelled.

He scrambled away from the bush. He hid behind the adjacent tree, his back against the trunk. Bullets hit the tree, chips of wood flying through the air. He covered his ears again, but he couldn't block out the gunfire. He wondered how many bullets it would take to cut down the tree—*a hundred? Two hundred? Five hundred?* It took less than fifty rounds to disintegrate Christina's body. He couldn't hide there forever.

He shouted, "I'm American! I'm a survivor! Don't shoot!" The bullets kept on hitting the tree. He cried, "Oh my God! Why?!"

"Ali! Ali!" a soldier shouted.

Over there! Over there!

The gunfire stopped hitting Nathan's cover. The soldiers turned their attention to an archer jumping from tree-to-tree in front of them. Some of the soldiers shot at him, others created a song of *clicks* and *clacks* as they reloaded their firearms. The archer fell from the tree as a branch broke under him. His ankle snapped as he landed on mud, his toes pointing behind him. He rolled down a hill towards the soldiers, reaching for every vine, bush, and flower in his path.

One after the other, the soldiers shot at him in a calm, organized order. The archer wasn't a threat without an aerial advantage. It was just a hunt to them. He was hit seven times before he reached the bottom of the hill. Then, a soldier walked up to his squirming body and shot him in the head twice—no prisoners, only executions.

Nathan seized the opportunity. He dashed away from the tree, keeping his head down. He ran behind the soldiers. *Behind enemy lines,* he thought, *but what if everyone's an enemy?* He heard some bullets whizzing past him, but he didn't hear any footsteps. After a minute of running, the gunfire faded away. They weren't following him.

"Where the hell am I going?" Nathan murmured.

Chapter Seventeen

In the Wilderness

Nathan waded across the creek. He gripped the chest of his shirt and coughed. He was out of breath, and each inhale sparked an inferno of pain in his chest. He needed oxygen to survive, but each breath made him want to die. He took a sip of water from the creek, then he dragged himself out and headed into the jungle on the other side.

"If I stop, I die," he whispered.

He didn't glance back, either. If he were to die, from an arrow or a gunshot, he didn't want to see it coming. Quick and easy, it was better that way.

He slid down a slope and followed a network of footprints—*bootprints.* He headed towards a group of killers. He witnessed their atrocious actions first-hand. An image of Christina's body flashed in his mind, but he couldn't recognize her. The bullets obliterated her frail body. He didn't have many other options, though. He hoped to find some Americans at their camp—military advisors, journalists, medics, *anyone.*

He walked past a tree, then he saw something from the corner of his eye. He staggered back behind the tree. He fought through the pain and took a deep breath through his nose. He peeked around the corner. His hands trembled, then his arms, and then his entire body. A mixture of fear and hope overwhelmed him. He couldn't tell if he stood on the porch of hell or heaven. In the jungle, it felt like everyone wanted to kill him.

He stumbled upon a field hospital. A wide, rectangular tan tent sat in the middle of an open field. A soldier stood guard outside of the front door, a rifle against his chest. Smaller, circular tents surrounded the tan tent. Soldiers and medics chatted near the tents while listening to the chatter from a radio. Their comrades kept them updated on the body count.

"Dez mortos, cara!"

Ten dead, man!

Weaving his head in every direction, Nathan whispered, "Who are these guys? Not Americans, no... Are they really here for us? Shit, what do I do?"

Sooner or later, the other soldiers would return. He witnessed the slaughter of indigenous people and the murder of an innocent woman. He was certain of only one thing: if they found him, they would kill him. He was a loose end after all. He sought answers and rescue. *The tent,* he thought, *if there are other survivors in there, maybe I can sneak in and blend in with them?*

He crawled out of the jungle and approached the side of the large tent. He pressed his chest against the wall of the tent, then he slid up slowly until he reached the window. He could see into the tent through the dirty vinyl window. Rows of beds hug the walls of the tents, but there were no patients inside. They hadn't found any survivors during their rescue operation. Only two men stood near the center of the tent: Francisco Silva and Davi Cardoso.

Francisco only wore a pair of boxer briefs. The wounds on his thigh and shoulder were cleaned and bandaged. Blotches of dark blood stained both bandages. He stood with the help of two crutches. He couldn't walk without them. Nathan leaned closer to the window. He furrowed his brow as he listened to their argument.

Francisco said, "Cardoso, I am begging you. We can *not* kill all of these people. That would be... It's genocide!"

"Genocide," Davi repeated, smirking. "I've heard words like those before, Mr. Silva, especially in the sixties and seventies. But I am not scared of labels or what you call 'genocide.' I am here to complete a job, and I *will* complete my job."

"Is it your job to... to... to slaughter dozens of innocent indigenous people? To–To make them extinct?"

Davi chuckled, then he said, "We are responding with force because *they* attacked us first. Look at yourself, Silva. You, yourself, are injured. Can't you see that?"

"I don't want them killed on my behalf. I've told you why they reacted like that. The deforesters and traffickers have been wiping out tribes in the area. They say they saw soldiers like you doing the same. They were only trying to protect themselves. This is... It's a misunderstanding."

"Misunderstanding or not, we must rescue the survivors of that crash. Our drones captured images of death and violence in that camp. You saw them yourself. If I can't rescue those innocent souls, then I will avenge them. That's the end of this discussion. You are dismissed."

Davi approached the exit, walking with excellent posture.

Teary-eyed, Francisco said, "This is wrong, Cardoso. I will tell this story to the media. *Everywhere.* The whole world will know what you did here."

Davi stopped near the exit. He stood there for fifteen seconds without saying a word or moving his head. He sighed in disappointment.

As he walked out of the tent, he said, "Pérez."

The guard marched into the tent. The name on his badge read: *Pérez.*

Francisco said, "O que você esta–"

The guard drew his handgun. At point blank range, he shot Francisco in the head, directly between the eyes. The anthropologist fell back like a fallen tree. The guard shot him through the heart, then through his head again. His precision was frightening. He was trained to execute.

Bug-eyed, Nathan gasped and tumbled down to his ass. Murder had a way of startling people. He crab-walked back to the jungle, leaving clouds of dirt in his wake. He slammed himself up against a tree and slapped his hands over his mouth. He was on the verge of panicking.

"Fuck, fuck, fuck," he said, his voice muffled by his own hands.

He heard footsteps near the field hospital. He looked down at his legs, then at his arms. *When did I start running?*–he thought. His fight-or-flight response took control of his body. It told him that he was safe *away* from people, so he sprinted into the jungle.

***

"Where to? Where to?" he asked himself. "Damn it, Nathan, where are you going?!"

He saw monkeys on the branches above him, moving in the same direction. He spotted a toco toucan sitting on a twig, its long orange beak glowing with the sunshine. Other birds chirped from the trees, playing music during the ongoing massacre. A few reptiles and rodents climbed trees and hid in the bushes. A large snake slithered across the mud, but he didn't bother to look at it. The snake's mere presence motivated him to run faster.

Nathan slid to a stop about three miles away from the field hospital. He glanced over his shoulder. An explosion echoed through the rainforest. The blast was loud and terrifying—louder than gunshots, scarier than shrieks of agony. Bombs were weapons of war and mayhem. They weren't supposed to be heard by civilian ears. He looked up at the sky, waiting for a fighter jet to fly by and drop a bomb on him.

He examined his surroundings. The birds stopped chirping, the wood stopped groaning, the leaves stopped rustling. It was an eerie moment of silence, as if the jungle had known about the casualties and destruction.

Nathan said, "This place... What is this place? Am I awake? Have I been dreaming this whole time?" As he ran off, he muttered, "It doesn't fucking matter. I can't die like this. I still have to tell their families about this. I am their closure. I owe them that. *At least.* I have to see Holly and Kyle again, too. There's so much I... Holy shit!"

He couldn't stop himself. He ran off a ledge. He landed on a patch of dirt one meter below, then he rolled down a steep hill. He crashed into bushes, tree trunks, and stones. His elbow was shattered, his forehead was sliced, and his ribs were cracked. He rolled for thirty-seven seconds before he stopped at the bottom of the hill. He groaned, lungs full of air, then he let out a painful exhale.

"Goddammit..."

A smile formed on his face. He saw the silhouette of a jaguar at the top of the hill.

"If I stopped, you would have mauled me. Huh? Maybe I'm alive because I have a guardian angel. Cole or maybe–"

He screamed as he felt a sharp pain in his ankle. Another jolt of pain came from the bottom of his foot. Then he felt it again around his ankle.

He shouted, "Oh my God!"

He wiggled on the ground and stared down at his right leg. He blinked rapidly, trying to focus his vision, but he wished he hadn't. He saw a Brazilian wandering spider chomping at his ankle. He spotted the legs of another spider behind his foot. He was hyperventilating before he knew it.

The hairy brown spiders had large two-inch bodies with six-inch leg spans. Their vibrant red jaws complemented their eight beady eyes. They were an arachnophobe's worst nightmare.

"No! No!" Nathan yelled.

He pulled the machete out and he swung it at the spider near his ankle. He chopped it in half with the first swing. He swung it at the other spider. He severed two of its legs, then he nearly cut its body in half. The spider tried to skitter away, but it tumbled within seconds. Before it could take another step, Nathan crushed the spider with a heavy rock. He slammed the rock against the other spider, too—for good measure.

He dragged himself away from the dead spiders, mumbling incoherently. He got on his hands and knees, crawled a meter forward, then he collapsed. He clawed his way to a tree, using vines and twigs to pull himself forward. He sat up and leaned back against the trunk. He breathed in short, panicked gasps. He couldn't catch his breath. He was surrounded by the freshest air, but it was all unsatisfying to him. He tore his shirt down the middle. He tapped his rosy chest and coughed.

Wheezing between each word, he said, "What... is... happening?"

He drank more water than the rest of the survivors thanks to his frequent visits to the creek, but he was still dehydrated. Yet, beads of sweat glimmered on his skin and dripped from his unkempt beard. Goosebumps spread across his arms, legs, and neck.

He figured he was poisoned by the spiders. He tried to pull his bitten foot up to his mouth. Although it wasn't recommended by doctors, he wanted to suck the venom out. He saw it in movies and TV shows about survival—suck and spit, suck and spit. He wasn't flexible enough, rolling from side to side.

After twenty minutes, his heartbeat accelerated and his head spun. He felt like a passenger prone to motion sickness on a boat, the mud under him rippling like waves. His vision became blurred. He couldn't see the spider bites on his foot and ankle. Then he saw double—two feet on one leg.

He chuckled nervously, then he said, "Oh, man, I'm fucked."

He grimaced and groaned as he looked at his crotch. His penis was stiff, harder than steel. He didn't feel any pleasure from it. The glans was sensitive and itchy while the shaft ached. He removed all of his clothes. He wiped the sweat off his body with his torn shirt. A fresh coat of sweat soaked him again within minutes.

He tried to find a logical solution to his problem. He began to masturbate. He used his sweat as lubricant. He thought about his wife at first—her firm breasts with those tiny pink nipples, her shaved crotch and brownish pussy. Her image brought sadness to his heart. So, he pictured the other female survivors instead. But he couldn't think about them without imagining their grisly wounds.

It didn't matter anyway. Each stroke amplified the pain. His penis was a blood-red smudge in his vision. Like the rest of his body, his dick was hotter than a curling iron. He wanted to ejaculate so the erection would end, but he couldn't finish.

He stuttered, "It–It's because of my–my leg. I need to–to stop the venom from spread–spreading."

Unbeknownst to him, the venom had already infiltrated his bloodstream and spread through his body.

He held the machete over his head, his arm swaying with the gentlest breeze. He blinked until he could see his kneecap. He took a deep breath, then he swung down at his leg. *Thud!*—the sound of steel hitting bone was unnerving. His tendons and ligaments emitted a *squishy* sound as he yanked the blade out. He gasped, then he held his breath.

"You can... do it."

He chopped at his leg again, but he missed his kneecap and sliced his shin. His tibia cracked. He swung down at himself again. He sliced into his knee, but he missed the first gash. He could barely see himself through his blurred vision. He saw the darkest reds and he felt the warmest blood on his leg. He kept chopping at himself, determined to amputate his leg.

After each swing, blood dripped from the blade and landed on his head, chest, and stomach, drizzled on him like chocolate on a cake. His mutilated flesh—muscles, ligaments, tendons—stuck out of the gashes. His leg shook involuntarily, performing a dance of its own. He couldn't sever his leg, although he was close. He sat in a puddle of his own blood, and the severe loss of blood rendered him anemic. His arms fell to his sides, limp.

His cries were raspy and his breathing was inconsistent. He gritted his teeth as he tapped his penis. He remained erect throughout the self-mutilation.

He said, "It's... because... it... hurts. I need to... to get rid of it."

He wasn't thinking straight. He grabbed the glans of his penis with a weak grip. He placed the edge of the machete against the shaft of his dick, then he sawed into it. The average penis required approximately four and a half ounces of blood to remain erect. He was longer and thicker than average, but not by much. Yet, he saw spurts of blood exploding out of his penis. Some of the blood even squirted out of his urethra.

By the time he severed his penis, he felt like he lost more than four and a half ounces of blood—more than five, more than six, *more than seven*. There was blood everywhere. His penis fell to the ground between his thighs, flaccid. The aching pain didn't stop, though. He moved his hand over his crotch, where his penis once stood like a tower of concrete. A squirt of blood burst out of his crotch and hit his palm.

He said, "It's gone, but... but I still feel it." He chuckled, but a coughing spell interrupted him. Smiling, he said, "I–I can–can't... be–believe this."

He couldn't comprehend the idea of *phantom pain.* His penis was gone, but the pain from the sore shaft and glans persisted. He leaned his head back against the tree. The coughing spasm continued. He stared up at the hill. He didn't see a jaguar anymore. He saw two human silhouettes, one taller than the other. He thought about Michael and Dylan, then he imagined a father and son from a tribe, and then he thought about his wife and son.

But he couldn't remember their names. He couldn't visualize them, either. Pain—*insufferable pain*—erased many of his memories. The venom didn't help. He knew he was married, though, and he knew he had a son.

"He's... waiting... for... me."

His head fell forward, bloody drool hanging from

his mouth and pooling on his stomach. His butchered leg stopped shaking. A few droplets of blood dripped out of the wound on his crotch, like water from a leaky faucet. His heart rate slowed to a crawl. He didn't feel his pulse in his arms or legs, as if the blood had stopped flowing through his body. He took a breath every fifteen seconds.

He heard Kyle's voice in his head: "When will you be back, dad?"

"I–I'll... be... ba–back... in..."

Nathan passed away against the tree.

Join the Mailing List!

Enjoy the book? Are you a fan of dark, disturbing horror novels? If so, you should sign up for my mailing list! I'm not planning a sequel to this book, but I've written several novels about cannibals in the past and I'm sure I'll write another one in the future. Most of my work is disturbing, violent, nasty, and provocative. Best of all: I release books very frequently!

By signing up for my mailing list, you'll be the first to know about my newest books, my *big* book sales, and other important news. You'll usually receive only one email per month. Sometimes you might receive two or three, sometimes you'll receive none. Either way, you have my word: I will *never* spam you. The process is fast, easy, and free, so visit this link to sign-up: http://eepurl.com/bNl1CP.

.

Dear Reader,

Thanks for reading *Cannibal Jungle.* This gory book was inspired by the cannibal horror movies of the 70s and 80s, such as *Cannibal Holocaust* and *Cannibal Ferox*. This probably isn't the first time I've mentioned this in one of these letters, but this book was also inspired by Jack Ketchum's *Off Season.* I'm a big fan of Ketchum and I highly recommend all of his work. So, with inspirations like this, it's no wonder this book ended up so gruesome and disturbing. I'm not sure if it's my most violent book to date, I don't really know how I'd keep track of that, but it's definitely up there. If you were offended by the contents of this book, try repeating this to yourself: *it's only a book, only a book, only a book.* (some people will get that reference.)

Cannibal Jungle was a difficult project. It took hours and hours of research, and I'm not sure if that was enough. You see, I'm not an anthropologist and I've never visited the Amazon rainforest. I didn't know much about the indigenous people of the region prior to writing this book, either. I suppose the news—as in, articles and broadcasts—planted the seeds of inspiration in my mind. Back in 2018, an uncontacted tribe was spotted by a drone in Brazil. Later that year, an American preacher was killed while trying to visit an uncontacted tribe on an island in India. I was fascinated by news like this. It made my mind run wild with ideas.

I didn't want to disrespect a real tribe in this book—my goal is to be provocative, not disrespectful—so I decided to leave them nameless. The book features some Spanish and Brazilian Portuguese. During the first draft, I actually wrote several lines of dialogue for the tribespeople using an indigenous language. But, again, I didn't want to connect this fictional tribe to a *real* group of people. On top of that, it was very difficult to write accurately in a language I didn't recognize. A single sentence took me nearly thirty minutes to translate, and I wasn't even sure if I wrote it correctly. So, that's why I didn't reference their language very much in this book.

I was skeptical of releasing this book with its first chapter. I *hated* writing the plane crash scene. I've always been scared of flying. *Final Destination* scarred me when I was around nine years old. In January 2019, I sucked it up and I boarded my first flight—and it wasn't so bad! In fact, during my flight back, I actually slept for several hours. However, news of planes falling from the sky shortly after takeoff reignited my aviophobia. That first chapter is supposed to be suspenseful and terrifying, but it's not supposed to be completely grounded in reality. I couldn't bring myself to write an ultra-realistic plane crash. I just couldn't do it.

The ending, however, was *a little* more realistic, even though it might seem a little 'out there.' Brazilian wandering spiders are terrifying. Unlike many other spiders, these are deadly, especially if you don't receive immediate medical attention. The venom from a Brazilian wandering spider also causes painful erections that last for hours. I had other plans for the ending, but I didn't want to drag it out. I also felt like this ending was the most unexpected. I wanted it to be a surprise in a shocking-but-humorous-type of way. As an arachnophobe and a man (yes, a man with a penis), it was also difficult to write. It's abrupt, I'd say it's even daring, but I hope you enjoyed it.

Okay, now it's time to beg for reviews. If you have time, *please* leave a review on Amazon.com. (Or Amazon.co.uk, Amazon.ca, or wherever you're from. I know I have some wonderful international readers out there!) Feel free to leave reviews on Goodreads and Bookbub, too. That's very helpful! Your reviews help me improve, they help me choose my next projects, and they help other readers find my books. When more people read my books, that gives me more resources to write more books—*better* books. It's not just about the money, either. Your reviews and your kind messages always motivate me. If it weren't for you, I wouldn't be doing this right now.

If you need help writing a review, try answering some of these questions: did you enjoy the book? Was it too disturbing, just right, or not violent enough for an extreme horror book? Were you satisfied by the ending? Would you like to read another book about cannibals in the future? Your review can be long and detailed or short and to the point. Regardless, it is *very* helpful.

I'm actually preparing myself for my second trip to Japan right now. I'll be away from April 19th to May 20th. Rest assured, this isn't just a long vacation. Yes, I will be spending time with my girlfriend, but I'll be working whenever she works. (She's Japanese, so she has a nine-to-five job there in Japan.) I'll be finishing up some novels that I've already started and I'll be planning some new projects. I'd love to write a story about Kuchisake-onna, also known as 'The Slit-Mouthed Woman.' I've been thinking about writing an extreme horror anthology about urban legends. I'd love to hear your opinion on that. Anyway, I have to thank you again for making this possible. If it weren't for your readership, I wouldn't be able to do things like this. I hope to repay you with some unforgettable books.

If you enjoyed this book, please visit my Amazon's author page and check out my other novels. I frequently release new books. I am an extreme horror author, but I've also written in the mystery, thriller, fantasy, supernatural, and sci-fi genres. Sometimes I mix them all together and try to create something new. Regardless of genre, my writing is always disturbing and provocative. What can I say? I enjoy being a provocateur. Last month, I released a book titled *The Taste of Blood.* It's about a teenage girl who believes she's a vampire—and she's willing to do anything to get some human blood. Next up, I'll be releasing a very disturbing horror/thriller about a cop who enlists a private investigator to help him find his kidnapped daughters. Thanks again for reading!

Until our next venture into the dark and disturbing,
Jon Athan

P.S. If you have any questions or comments, or if you're an aspiring author who needs *some* help, feel free to contact me directly using my business email: info@jon-athan.com. You can also contact me through Twitter @Jonny_Athan or my Facebook page.

Made in the USA
Las Vegas, NV
27 April 2024